I0684475

SATI AND THE CLOVER

A Satyana Mystery

Winslow Eliot

Vol II

Visit the author website: winsloweliot.com

Cover design: Tom Stier – tomstier.com

Cover art: Carrie Paris – carrieparis.com

Author website created by promoteglobally.com

Author photo by Sarah Dinan

ISBN: 978-1-939980-12-0 (paperback)
ISBN: 978-1-939980-13-7 (kindle)
ISBN: 978-1-939980-14-4 (epub)
ISBN: 978-1-939980-15-1 (audio)
Published by: Writespa Press – writespa.com

Grateful thanks to Sheilaa Hite, Maria Rivera, and all my other Odyssey travelers for our inspiring adventures in Scotland.

The Clover:
Luck, joy, a pleasant surprise.
Enjoy the good fortune while it lasts.
An auspicious time or event. A fluke.
6 of Diamonds: Good news, luck, good fortune.
Timing: Now, fleeting.

 My last client for the day was a plus-size, pretty woman in her mid-thirties, with a nervous habit of scratching the backs of her hands when she talked to me. Maybe she had eczema or psoriasis, but I wished she'd wear gloves.

I'd met Amber Witherspoon—that was her name—the previous week at a small art gallery in Brooklyn. I'd been drawn by three smallish landscape paintings hanging in the window. The center one was of an ancient stone circle, pierced in its center by a rich beam of light emanating from somewhere behind dark clouds.

Curious about it, I'd entered the Thistle Gallery. Amber had greeted me apologetically, emerging from an office at the far side of the wide room, explaining in a timid voice that seemed incongruous with her size that everyone else was out and she was the only one there. She said she was 'just' the bookkeeper, and she was new.

I told her I was interested in the painting in the window. "What's it of?" I asked.

She repeated she was just the bookkeeper and she'd only recently started. "It's by McCoy Brown, I think." Gingerly, she lifted it out of the window and peered at the signature in the corner. "Yes. It's by him."

Then she handed it to me. The painting was small, no more than twelve inches high, framed in simple dark wood. I turned it over and saw written on the back, in slanting, jagged letters: *Croft Moraig, 1969.*

As I studied the painting again, a longing pulsed through me. The ancient stones seemed to tremble and glow. The painting was so very sweet!

"How much is it?" I asked, impulsively.

Nervously, she went over to the computer on the receptionist's desk. "I should have the owner of the gallery call you."

"I'm just curious," I lifted my rapt gaze from the painting and smiled reassuringly.

She tapped some keys. "It says here $999."

I was astonished—the painting seemed much more valuable.

I wanted it. On the other hand, that was a lot of money for me.

"I'd better ask the owner to call you," Amber said, staring at the price on the screen as though she too found it hard to believe.

At the same time I heard myself saying, "I'll take it."

Amber looked excited that she'd made a sale when

it clearly wasn't her job, but she was obviously also worried that she might be doing the wrong thing. Before she could demur, I paid for the painting and handed her one of the lovely new business cards Percy had designed for me. It was much more elegant than anything I'd had before: besides my name and contact information in cursive pink, it featured an alluring cocoa-colored armchair that enticed you to sit in it and ask me questions.

"You're a psychic?" she'd gushed, looking at it.

I nodded. "Come and see me sometime," I said while she carefully wrapped the painting in tissue, bubble wrap, and brown paper.

Then the next day Percy said an Amber Witherspoon had called to make an appointment to see me for a psychic consultation.

And so here we were.

Her question had to do with a budding romance: She wanted to know more about the owner of the Thistle Gallery. According to her, he was successful, charming, handsome, and, although she didn't say so out loud, she was obviously smitten by him.

But was *he* as fond of *her*? I studied the cards laid out on the velvet cloth in front of us and felt that yes, he probably was. All the evidence of strong passion was there, not just in the many cups that had shown up and in the madly swinging pendulum that I used to assess his energy, but also in the fact that she told me he wanted to take her to Scotland for a romantic vacation. Turned out, he was Scottish, a U.S. transplant.

But for some reason Amber wasn't telling me, she

was nervous about dating him. I had the sense there was something about him she wasn't sure she could trust. Her out-loud question was: *Does he really love me?* But her unasked question seemed more important.

I wished I knew what it was.

"Tell me more about him," I said, scooping up the cards and handing the deck to her. "Here, shuffle. Is he your age?"

"I think so." She sat stiffly as she tried to push the cards into each other. A purple and black contessa skirt poured from her waist to her rubber boots that were still shiny from the rain. She'd tucked a bright blue and rose silk scarf around her shoulders. Everything about her looked normal, except the way her eyes darted around the room, evasively. I knew she was not asking me her real question.

She handed me back the cards.

I closed my eyes, took several deep breaths, and grew still. Sometimes I just couldn't be sure my intuition was working. It wasn't that I doubted the cards—it was that I doubted myself.

But when the cards were laid out in front of me, their message was so clear I stared, astonished.

Her potential Scottish romance didn't only look unromantic, but *dangerous*.

 I rarely use that word in my readings because it tends to make people nervous, but the warning clamored like a loud bell in my head. While I tried to buy some time, Amber looked around my little office, as though seeking something.

There wasn't much to explore. It was a smallish room, with tall windows overlooking a handkerchief-sized garden at the back. Spring rain spattered loudly on the glass panes. There was a sideboard where I kept some books and cards, but most of my fortune-telling accoutrements were stored in the oak chest that doubled as a low table I used for card readings.

"Where did you say he's from?"

"Scotland. I had a great-grandmother from there. I feel we're connected, sort of."

"Where did you work before the Thistle?"

"I was an accountant. In Queens. I'm from there."

"How did you get this job?"

She wouldn't look at me. "Heard about it through a friend. When Robert interviewed me, he wanted to hire me right away. I know it's just temporary, but I really need the money."

I glanced at the cards. "Have you been dating someone else?"

"No."

"But there's another man in your life?"

She looked at me with a scared expression. "Not— *romantic*. Is that what you mean?"

I glanced at the cards again, wondering why

Amber didn't want to be candid. "Not necessarily. But there *is* someone who is influencing your feelings about your new boss in some way."

She looked at me with something like awe, so I knew I'd nailed something… I *wished* I knew what it was.

"I know he likes me. A lot. I don't think he's lying about that."

"But you don't feel the same way about him?"

"Well, I do like him." She spoke softly as she scratched.

"I see." I tried to get the sense of danger into some sort of perspective. Maybe I was making it up. It wasn't that the cards themselves were ominous—it was a feeling I had. "Who else works at the gallery?"

Amber scratched again. "Just Kathleen—she's the office manager." She was nervous and twitchy and still found it hard to meet my eyes. But her large oval face, with dark eyes, was hauntingly lovely. Her lips gleamed with a wildflower gloss, and her small teeth were straight and even. If she'd only wear gloves…

She looked around the room again and her eyes rested on the McCoy painting that I'd hung over the fireplace mantel, replacing an old painting Leandros had made of a Maine lighthouse. Even though this one was much smaller, its presence was intense. "Oh, there it is," she said absently.

I wondered whether she'd tell me the painting was worth ten times what I'd paid for it, and that she wanted me to return it so she wouldn't get into trouble. But by this time I loved it so much I was loathe to part with it, even for Amber's sake.

"So there are only four of you who work there?"

"Yes, Robert likes to handle pretty much everything himself. Even the books. He's showing me how he wants me to…" She flushed. "I'm learning so much from him."

"Have you ever had a serious relationship before now?"

"Not really," she answered. "I was living with my parents up till a few years ago. There was someone from high school who liked me. Sort of."

"But did you like him?"

"Not really."

"But you really like this new person…Robert?"

She looked surprised, as though that wasn't as important as the fact that he liked her. Her self-esteem issues ran deep.

"It seems to me that your real question is not about whether or not Robert is the man of your dreams, but about your own heart. What is it saying to you?"

"What do you mean?"

"How do you feel about him?" I paused. "He makes you nervous, doesn't he? You don't seem comfortable around him."

Amber flushed again and tears welled in her pretty blue eyes. "I don't know."

"Does he give you lots of gifts? Things that make you feel extra-lucky… he's generous, right?"

"Y—es." She spoke very slowly. "He brings me fresh flowers for my desk practically every day."

"So he's not married? No other girlfriend?"

"No. Well, there *was* a girlfriend, but that's all over. At least, he says it is. He says he's in love with me. That this might be the real deal. That means marriage, doesn't it? Maybe?"

I glanced at the cards again, trying vainly to see something encouraging.

But there was nothing even close to marriage in her forecast.

I went on gazing at the cards. I had to pull myself out of the feeling of hopelessness. Even when an outcome seemed inevitable, I never made predictions, since I've learned there are too many variables involved to be sure about what someone might do with my advice. Everyone can make their own choices—that's the point of human beings having free will.

She scratched again. "Tell me, please, can I trust him?"

"Trust him how?" I asked.

"You know—you *must* know—"

So far this consult had gone on for forty-five minutes, and soon Percy, my ultra-assistant, was going to remind me that our time was up. He was strict about not making my next client wait. He was also vigilant about giving me at least a few minutes to clear the air in between my consulting sessions.

So I knew I had to wrap this up, even though it wouldn't be easy. But people can always make a change in their lives, and alter the course of where they're headed, so I needed to help her as best I could.

"I can see you think you're in love," I said. "And

he seems to have strong feelings for you as well."

Her skin flushed a delicate pink again. "He *says* he does." She sounded embarrassed. "But—" She stopped.

"Why wouldn't he be attracted to you? You're beautiful and smart."

She got even pinker. "I just don't know whether I can trust him."

"Why not?"

"He makes these promises…" She stared at her reddened hand as though it didn't belong to her.

"What kinds of promises? Marriage?"

"No—not yet. About…" she swallowed. "Other things. Like—money. My salary…"

I wished she'd be more open. "When did you meet? Was it recently?"

"I started working at the Thistle Gallery two weeks ago."

That seemed very fast, both for a new romance and *any* sort of promise. You didn't have to be intuitive to feel that this was rushed.

"I'm getting the sense that it would be wise to take things slow with him," I said. "Is there a reason to hurry?"

"Yes, because he wants to take me to Edinburgh for two weeks. I really want to go. That's where my grandparents were from. But should I?"

"There's no 'should' about it," I said gently. "You need to follow your own heart. But I do advise you to move slowly with him. Can you go on this trip in a few months? How about later this summer? Things will be different then."

"I don't think so."

"Why not?"

"He might not like me any more by then."

I wanted to give Amber a little lecture on liking herself, but restrained myself, knowing that the session had to come to an end.

"I don't see the pleasure in going now, if the relationship is so uncertain."

"He says he'll pay for everything..."Again she hesitated. "I don't get opportunities like this, ever. I might never have another one. Don't you think I should risk it?"

Clearly she'd already made up her mind, and nothing I said would change it. But I had to warn her.

"I know on the surface it sounds good. But there's something very short-lived about the relationship. I think you need to get to know each other better first, really find out more about him."

She seemed startled by my advice. "Not go with him?" A flash of anger crossed her eyes. She scratched her hand furiously and I longed to loan her a pair of cotton gloves that I always kept in a drawer. "Are you *kidding* me?"

So she had definitely already made up her mind. Then why had she bothered to consult with me?

"I'm telling you what I'm—"

"You don't know what you're talking about!" Amber snapped, leaping to her feet.

She was a good four inches taller than me, and I'm not short. Her skirt swirled around her rubber boots. The cards were swept from the oak chest and fluttered to the floor. A few even reached where Leandros's painting stood, facing the wall in the corner.

I gestured to them. "I'm only telling you that –"

"Shut up—*shut up!*" She was practically crying with rage as she towered over me.

Strange.

I was glad Percy arranged it so that all my clients paid before our session, not after. I had a strong feeling that she wouldn't be interested in paying for this one now.

She looked around for her silver vinyl tote bag, which she'd placed on the floor by the sideboard. I bent over to begin gathering the spilled cards.

"You're a *fraud!*" her voice squeaked, her back to me, hunched over the mantel. "I *knew* it! Everything you've told me is *crap*. Just crap. You don't know what you're talking about. I *knew* you didn't."

 The tranquil sound of the singing bowl floated through the closed door: it was Percy's signal that our time was up. I gathered up the last of the cards, set everything back on the chest, and got to my feet. Amber was turned away from me, her shoulders shaking with anger. Was she crying?

"Are you all right?" I asked.

I saw the back of her head nod, and then she gulped, "Sorry… It's just—that's not what I thought you would say."

"It doesn't feel like the right time to make a major commitment," I said as gently as I could. I went to the door and held it open. "Why don't you wait a week or so and see what happens? There's no real rush, you know."

She nodded, looking at me through pleading, teary eyes, as though there *was* a rush, but she didn't say anything. Tote bag in hand, she pushed past me to the outer office, where Percy was watering the philodendron beside the window that overlooked Gay Street. I hung back as she slid her large frame out the front door, then joined Percy in picking off some dead leaves from the plant.

He glanced up at me with a cheerful grin. "Trouble in paradise?"

"You heard?"

"Not too much. Just her screech near the end. What did you tell her?"

"Just to take things slowly. She didn't like hearing that. Definitely an unsatisfied client."

"Her problem, not yours." Even though Percy shrugged, I knew he was concerned about me.

I reassured him. "I'm okay, but thanks."

His warm brown eyes smiled back. "Why'd she come for advice if she didn't want to hear it?"

I sighed. "I have a feeling that's not what she really came to ask me about. Her question wasn't about a boyfriend, not really. There was something else…and, oh, it's just so frustrating that I can't just *know* these things."

"Oh, you know all right," he said, diffidently.

He could always lift my spirits. "Thanks."

"Your next appointment cancelled."

"Oh, well." I was relieved Amber was my last client for the day. I needed more than just a few minutes to recover from the immense gray cloud that lingered behind.

He returned to his chair behind the pristine desk, checked something on his open laptop, then closed it. "Ready to go out?"

Percy had shown up literally on my doorstep during the winter, delivering a package. He'd fallen, broken his ankle, and one thing had led to another. Now, even though he was only in his mid-twenties, he had become the best personal assistant I could ever imagine. He'd found several repeat clients for me and he managed all the financial bits of the business, and in return he got a portion of my salary. I was gradually becoming so successful that I wanted to increase his percentage. But he wanted to wait until six months went by, to make sure our success was not a fluke.

"Besides, business might be slow in summer. Better wait."

I had told him he was way too young to commit to working in a business that didn't take him to lots of glamorous places and didn't involve meeting exciting young people—especially women his own age—but he said he preferred working for me. Since I had recently (and quietly) celebrated my forty-ninth birthday, I didn't take his crush too seriously. But sometimes I caught him looking at me with an expression that concerned me.

It was Sunday evening, which for me was the end of the workweek. Percy arranged all my consultations so that I had Mondays and Tuesdays off, so my Sundays were like most other peoples' Fridays. I felt relaxed and satisfied after a good week of work.

We had gotten in the habit of going out for dinner on Sunday nights and chatting about how the week went. Our favorite place was a Mexican dive not too far from where I live in Greenwich Village. But tonight I suggested we take the subway to Dumbo, in Brooklyn. There was a new vegetarian place I wanted to try.

Percy was always amenable to trying something new, but he knew that was not the real reason I wanted to go to Dumbo.

"What's the name of the gallery where she works?"

"The Thistle Gallery."

Within an hour we were strolling along Front Street. The usual parade of chic artists, fashionistas, and tourists was thin at this time of year, but it was still busy. Lights from lower Manhattan twinkled across the river. This late March evening was a little warmer than it had been in a while, and my cloak kept me snug and my boots were made for slush. I was pretty happy. We gazed at the springtime-decorated windows, not talking very much, enjoying each other's company.

I was thinking that Percy was the best thing that ever happened to me.

We arrived at the street where I'd come across the gallery the week before and peered in the darkened, gated window. Now the painting in the middle of the threesome, replacing the one I'd bought, was of a surging coastal seascape.

Percy crossed the street and stood on the sidewalk across from the building, looking up. I joined him. It was a five-story brownstone, with the fire escape plunging down from the roof to the first floor, painted a terracotta red. All the lights were off, except for a pale fluorescent flicker in a room on the fourth floor.

As we watched, we saw the silhouette of a large woman framed in the single lit room. She seemed to tower over a slighter figure. What were they doing?

Arguing?

As we watched, it seemed as though the slighter figure lifted his arm and struck the side of the woman's head. But it was hard to tell for sure.

His silhouette moved away from the window frame. Then she left it, too.

 We hung around for a few minutes, not sure what to do. Percy finally convinced me to go have dinner. What we saw might have been nothing, or it might have been a benign lovers' quarrel. Percy suggested it might even have been an affectionate exchange.

It was not till the following afternoon, when I was heading upstairs to make myself tea, that Percy said, "That's interesting."

I paused, my hand on the banister. "What is?"

"The numbers for the Cloverleaf Lottery were just announced. We didn't win."

"Percy, you didn't really expect we would, did you?

"No, but it's always fun to look. It was almost at $2 million. One can always hope."

"Sure one can."

Percy was a genius in many ways, but his fascination with the lottery seemed absurd to me. He claimed he was interested purely as a statistical phenomenon, but in my opinion he was way too serious about it. He was convinced there was a way to beat the system.

Maybe there was, but so far it hasn't happened to us. I had no faith at all that one of the pale green little tickets he bought each week, with the small cloverleaf on the left side, and a grinning, winning smile in its leaf-framed face, would ever bring me out of debt.

"If no one's claimed the winning ticket by a week from Friday—that's the end of the month—they'll distribute the two million between the next level of wins. But we still won't be in the running."

"There's a cap?"

"Yep, they cap it at two million. That's why it's not as popular as the ones that keep pouring the un-won funds back into the pool. But it's also more likely we might get at least something back."

I told him I was all in favor of distribution of wealth at whatever level, and he grinned at me.

Of course I knew he wasn't telling me about the lottery winners because he thought I was interested. I thought all lotteries were swindles. "So what's this all about?" I asked.

"I was looking back over the past year's winners. The owner of the gallery—Robert McNeil—has won several times. There've been news stories about how he's managed that."

Okay, now *that* I was definitely interested in. I

came back down the stairs.

Percy did a little more investigating while I waited, then looked up.

"Another repeated winner is someone called Kathleen Jones."

"She works at the gallery too. Amber said she's the office manager." I mulled. "Maybe the employees there pool their tickets. Increases their chances of winning?"

"Maybe." He frowned. "Statistically, it seems impossible that this one guy would've won so often. And your client, Amber, hasn't won anything before. But she just started there, right?"

"A couple of weeks ago."

"Well, let's hope if they do win something this week, she gets to be part of it."

"She's very new at the firm—maybe it takes a while to be asked to join the pool."

"That would be a bummer, wouldn't it? To miss out on a win?"

"Could be the end of a beautiful friendship."

Percy stretched, tipping his chair way back. "Well, let's hope we don't ever win so that won't happen to us."

Just the way he looked at me made me feel young and jaunty. I tucked my hands into the big pockets of my merino sweater and went on upstairs, wondering vaguely whether Amber had decided to go to Scotland with her new lover, or if she'd decided it was too fast, and too soon.

I made myself a cup of tea at four—today's was a rose-scented Assam—and then tackled a cardigan I was trying to knit. At six-thirty I went to visit my elderly friend Judy at her apartment near the East River. I used to go on Saturdays, but now my consulting schedule was so filled on weekends that I went there on Mondays instead. Judy had been a friend some years ago, but it was only since I'd moved back to New York City that we'd rekindled our friendship. She'd written a book on the seven rays of the human dimension back in the 1970s, and she had been an inspiration from the time I met her when I was in my teens.

Even now, although she didn't leave her little rent-controlled apartment in a high-rise near the East River, she was spry and bright-eyed. I thought of her as my lodestone—a person I knew I could be near and who would always remind me of who I was.

Today she teased me, as she always did, about my feeling that I'd lost my psychic gift. It had happened over a year ago, after a strange event in the Berkshires. An encounter had catapulted me into a high-profile, very unpleasant media sensation, and the safe confines of the mountains, woods, and small New England village in which I had thought I had found peace at last became a nightmare. Ever since then, I felt unable to tap into my intuitive power the way I always had up till then.

Looking back now, I knew life was pushing me in another direction, and trying to get me ready for my next move. And several months later, a client who appreciated something I'd done for her many years earlier died unexpectedly and left me her Greenwich Village brownstone in New York City. I'd moved in right away. People thought I was incredibly lucky, which I was, but at the same time the challenge of finding enough money to pay the inheritance tax, the property tax, and to fix a leaking roof (which I still hadn't done) and do other necessary repairs took a huge toll on my health and mood.

Judy had encouraged me to go on offering divination consultations, and to trust that I'd be offering the right words and guidance, even though it didn't seem to be coming from the same place it used to.

Not having any other skill to take its place, I'd taken her advice and set up my consulting business in Greenwich Village. Then Percy had shown up, and turned my business around.

"Has it come back yet?" Judy asked.

I shook my head.

"Don't worry. It will – just when you least expect it."

I'd brought hummus pita sandwiches, with grape leaves and babaganoush, from a nearby Mediterranean restaurant, and I unwrapped them for us as we chatted. Judy was reading a new book by Pema Chödrön, so we mostly talked about that.

I also told her about my new purchase. "It's a gorgeous oil painting of a stone circle called Croft Moraig. I looked it up—it's located in Scotland. I fell in love with it. And I couldn't believe it was only $1,000. I looked up the artist, and his paintings usually sell for a lot more."

"What era?"

"Late 1960s. The artist must have painted it soon

after it was discovered. It's beautiful—but it's more than that. It feels mystical."

When I got back to 22 Gay Street it was already nine o'clock and a chill spring wind had risen. I took out my key as I neared my house.

I noticed a man sitting on my stoop, looking like he was waiting for someone. He wore a greyish suit, and a baseball cap shadowed the top part of his face.

There was no light in Percy's basement apartment, so he was probably out somewhere with his friends.

I paused. It was going to be awkward pushing past him to get to my front door. Our eyes might have met, but because of the baseball cap and the dark I couldn't tell.

The wind blew again.

"Excuse me," I said, and placed my boot on the first step.

The man stood up, barring my way. "Are you Satyana?" he demanded in a strangely soft voice.

"Yes."

"I need to talk to you."

I arched an eyebrow and frosted my voice. "What is it?"

"Can I come in?" His voice was lilting and mellifluous, in spite of its urgency. "It's really important."

No way. I was not going to invite a total stranger into my house at nine o'clock at night.

He was a slight man, and his faintly-Scottish

accent was like a breeze on the sea. His chin was smooth, his lips thin. But I couldn't see his eyes.

I knew by this time who it was: Amber's Scottish romance. I lifted my chin and cooled my voice even more. "Sorry, you'll have to make an appointment."

"The woman who came to see you two days ago — Amber — where is she? Is she all right?"

I frowned. "What do you mean?"

"I'm Robert McNeil. She works for me. *And* I'm also a good friend of hers." He stepped down so we were at eye level. Now his face was completely in shadow. "I need to speak with her. I think there might be a misunderstanding…"

I studied him curiously but shook my head.

"I'm sorry, I don't discuss my clients' consultations with anyone. Why don't you ask her yourself?"

"Because she's disappeared. Hasn't shown up at the office, either. And she won't answer my calls."

I tried to gauge him. Was this the person who had struck her the previous evening? I couldn't tell.

"I'm sorry I can't help you."

"Wait." He actually grabbed a handful of my cloak to stop me. I wished the light was on in Percy's basement apartment. Gay Street was very quiet that early spring evening.

"What did you tell her?" he demanded.

I was silent, waiting for him to let go.

"Do you have any idea where she might be?"

"No, I don't. Goodnight."

"It's extremely important I find her."

"If she contacts me again, I'll tell her you're

looking for her."

He glared starkly. "Aren't you worried about her? I'm telling you, she's disappeared."

I didn't like hearing this. "Tell the police."

"They won't help me." He wouldn't let go of my cloak. "I have nothing to go on—there's nothing I can tell them. But I think she might be dead."

 With my gloved hand, I extricated his fingers from my cloak. As I touched him, even through my gloves I could sense a very real despair. Was he really worried about Amber? I didn't go inside yet. "Why do you think that?"

"She didn't come into work these past two days, she's not at her apartment, she's not answering any calls or texts. We're *friends*—actually, we're more than that. I *know* she wouldn't disappear without telling me."

Studying him, I wondered about that. Was this really the man she'd fallen so hard for?

I reached into the pocket of the lining of my cloak, took out a business card, and handed it to Robert.

"Call that number in the morning and make an appointment if you'd like to talk with me. But my advice is that you get in touch with the police if you're worried."

I inserted the key in the door, and quickly went inside. It swung closed behind me and I slid the bolt across. Thankfully, Robert hadn't made any attempt to push his way in after me.

I stood in the dark for a moment, then peered through the beveled glass panes beside the front door. He was still there, his thin face pressed against the glass, staring back at me.

I backed away hastily so that I was out of sight.

The reception area was lit by the street light, which shone through the translucent linen drapes in the bay windows overlooking the street. The desk was immaculate, as usual. Percy managed to do all his work on his computer or his phone, so I rarely had piles of papers strewn around, as there used to be before he had shown up in my life. The ottoman was neatly placed between the two fine scissor chairs, three issues of *New Yorkers* neatly fanned on top.

Everything seemed in order.

But it wasn't.

Something made me feel uneasy, and not just the stranger on the stoop. I didn't know what it was—a faint rustle or a creaking floorboard, or maybe just the awareness that someone else was close by.

My office, at the back of the small house, was in pitch dark. The thicker drapes in there kept out any light that might have filtered in from the little garden.

Then I actually heard something, sort of like a faint intake of breath.

Now I was certain of it: *Someone was in my office.*

My first instinct was to shove back the bolt and hightail it back out onto the street. But the stranger — Robert—was still standing out there.

Very quietly, I took off one of my velvet gloves and tiptoed along the edge of the wall toward the open office door. Then I slid my hand around the edge of the wall so the palm was facing into the dark room, while I still stayed out of sight.

My hand turned this way and that, peering around like an old-fashioned periscope. It had been a long time since I used this technique of seeing without using my eyes. I had been taught the skill by an old yogi when I lived in India, many years ago. He had shown me that we can 'see' with any organ, especially our skin. It was a sixth sense that we all have, akin to knowing when someone is watching us, even if our backs are turned to them. Most people don't have the time to practice enough and hone it to usefulness. Or they don't believe in it. By the end of the two years I'd spent with him, I'd learned how to sometimes be able to see simply by using the palm of my hand.

Still staying completely out of the doorway, I continued to move my palm. It didn't see like my eyes did, straining into the dark, trying to figure out who was there. Using a palm was different. There was no dark or light—there was just clarity. I sensed someone almost right away, standing in front of the chocolate drapes, face drawn, eyes wide and frightened.

I stayed out of sight.

"Hi, Amber," I said quietly.

 She gasped loudly. My hand changed purpose and reached for the switch. In an instant the room was flooded with light. I stepped into the doorway, still in my cloak, so I was silhouetted by the streetlight from Gay Street.

"What are you doing here?"

Amber dove behind the sofa, cowering behind it.

"He'll see me!" she hissed hysterically. "Turn it off!"

I glanced behind me, but couldn't see from here if the stranger was still waiting on my stoop.

"What are you doing here?" I asked unsympathetically. "How did you get in?"

"Please turn off the light," she begged. "Don't let him see me!"

I turned on a softer lamp on a side table, and switched off the overhead. Then I closed the office door so that even if Robert McNeil stood on the stoop on the other side of the street, he wouldn't be able to see inside the office.

A bit clumsily because of her weight and the spindly heels, Amber pulled herself up and stood behind the couch, facing me with frightened eyes. A short, tight jacket made of blue velvet was bunched around her waist, making her appear larger than she was. She tried to straighten it, and then pushed down the too-tight navy pencil skirt around her hips. On her nylon-clad feet she wore spindly dark blue high heels, with tiny crystal buckles.

She reached for her silver tote bag that was propped on the couch and clutched it defensively in front of her.

"Okay, tell me what you're doing here," I demanded. "First of all, how did you get in?"

She trembled, scratched the backs of her hands and behind her ears. "Your assistant let me in. He said you'd be back soon."

Whoa! *Percy* let her in?

Not likely. There was no way Percy would leave one of my clients alone in my house without one of us being there.

"Tell me the truth," I said. "How did you get in?"

Her black eyes filled. "I—I took that key from the basket by the front door when I was leaving yesterday. Your assistant didn't see me do it."

I'd placed a basket by the front door because there'd been too many times in the past when I'd inadvertently dashed outside and the front door closed behind me, locking me out. This way I always automatically grabbed a key before heading out in a hurry. I'd thought it was a good system. But apparently it wasn't.

"Why?" When she didn't answer, I demanded: "Why did you want to sneak back in here like this? Why not just make an appointment to see me?"

"I'm afraid. That man I told you about—Robert— he's going to kill me. I *know* he is. I'm sure he knows I'm here. He's waiting for me. He'll kill me."

I decided not to tell her he'd hinted she might already be dead. She was already so nervous I thought she might faint. I told her to sit on the couch then I asked, "Has he hurt you? Threatened you?"

"Not—exactly."

"Then why are you hiding? Why do you think he wants to kill you?"

"He's crazy. He's so jealous—he wants me to go to Scotland with him—"

I heard the gate to the basement apartment clang shut.

Percy was back! I felt *much* better. I opened the office door a crack and could hear him telling Robert to move along.

"*Please* don't make me go outside," Amber begged. "Please let me stay here. Just for one night. Tomorrow I'll be gone, I promise."

"If you're being harassed or threatened, let's call the police. He'll be arrested and maybe you can get a restraining order. He *has* hurt you, hasn't he?"

Her eyes widened and watered again. "Oh, *no*. *Please* don't call the police!"

"Why not? They'll protect you."

"No—*no*." She seemed so upset that I was worried about her.

While I went to get her a glass of water to calm her down, I debated my options:

Make her leave immediately and to hell with what happened to her.

Text Percy and ask what he thought I should do.

Call the police—after all, she was an intruder.

Let her stay.

I couldn't make her leave without feeling responsible for what might happen to her, and that was why I decided not to call the police either. I mean, they could be protective and helpful—but only up to a point. Most likely, they wouldn't believe she was in any danger, and they'd make her go home. Alone.

If I texted Percy I knew he'd insist on the same thing.

So I opted for letting her stay, curious about why she was so frightened. I watched her sip the water and recover her poise a little. "What's going on, Amber?

Tell me the truth."

She gulped, choked, then said very softly: "My parents are in trouble…my dad got sick and they haven't been able to pay the medical bills. They had to refinance their house and then they borrowed even more money."

"Go on."

"I've tried to help out. It's taken me forever to get a job. I taught myself bookkeeping, but I'm not really good at it. I lied about the diploma I said I'd gotten online. When Robert offered me the job I was so relieved, but if he finds out I lied…"

"I'm sure he wouldn't kill you over that," I pointed out. "Wouldn't it be simpler just to fire you?"

She stared with wide eyes. "He's promised me money…that would really help out my dad…"

So Robert was enticing her with visions of sugarplums because he had a crush on her. And maybe he was for real. He'd certainly seemed anxious about her outside on the stoop.

But why was she afraid he might kill her?

"Has he threatened you in some way?" I demanded. "Or hit you?"

"N-no. But if he found out that—I think Kathleen—she works at the gallery too. She might have told him—"

"Told him what?"

"Just that—I don't know if I can trust him. He gets so angry."

I regarded her for a long moment, feeling abruptly weary.

"Okay, you can sleep here on the couch. I'll bring

you a throw, but it stays pretty warm. We'll talk this over tomorrow and decide what's best. You know where the bathroom is, under the stairs?"

She nodded. The way she looked at me, I realized she'd already explored the house. Feeling a little creeped out, I almost opted for calling the police again, but her truly sad eyes stopped me. I hoped she didn't go all the way to the top floor; it was always hard for me to sleep if someone's been in my bedroom.

I decided to sleep on the couch on the second floor instead. It was supposed to rain anyway, so I'd be better off there instead of under the leaky roof.

"Thank you so, *so* much." Her pale face was getting some of its color back.

I mellowed. "You'll be safe here. Tomorrow we'll talk about getting you some sort of protection. I know a detective down at the precinct who'll advise us what to do, okay?"

She nodded gratefully.

I got her a soft throw and handed her one of the couch pillows, then closed the office door. Before going up the stairs, I peered through the glass beside the front door but there was no one on the stoop now. The bolt was secure; I checked the back door as well.

It was well and truly locked.

 I awoke to the sound of pouring rain. Tying the sash around my green dressing gown, I looked out the window. Gay Street looked glistening and clean. Quentin was organizing

the trash barrels — it was trash collection day.

Then I remembered: *Amber*.

Percy would be coming to the office soon. Even though it was officially our day off, he liked to check in with me and make sure there were no pressing details to take care of. He usually came in the back way, through the garden, and used the back door key, then unbolted the front door, checked my day's schedule, and made sure everything was in order.

I texted him to warn him that someone was sleeping in my office and not to be surprised.

His response was a terse "*ok*."

I was still sipping an Irish breakfast tea when I heard the back door close. Then he called me instead of texting.

"There's no one here, Sati," he said. "And the back door was unlocked when I came in."

"So she's gone?"

"Who was 'she'?"

"Amber — that client from two days ago. Wait a sec, I'm coming down."

I hurried downstairs. My brownstone was three stories, plus the basement apartment where Percy lived. The reception and office, where I consulted with clients, was on the first floor. The second floor, where I spent most of my time, was one largish room that included a galley kitchen, a small dining table, and a couch. The top floor was partly a tiny bedroom with a leaky roof and the rest a lovely terrace.

Since Percy's arrival in my life, we had done a lot of fixing up of the first floor, where I met my clients, but I hadn't done much to alter the rest of the house. I knew I needed to. I'd moved in last fall, but so much had happened over the six months that I hadn't had time to put my mind to interior designing.

Wearing a dark blue t-shirt and sweatpants, Percy was sliding back the bolts on the front door but left it locked, looking perturbed.

"The front door was bolted, so she must have left through the garden."

I went into my office. Everything seemed the same. The chest was shut, and the Chinese vase with some dried flowers was in exactly the same place I'd left it. The McCoy painting was over the mantel and Leandros's painting of the lighthouse was in the corner, facing the wall. There was no sign I'd had a visitor last night, except for the folded throw neatly placed on the sofa arm.

"You let a complete stranger spend the night in your office?" Percy reproved, following me.

"She claimed that man who was on our stoop last night was threatening her. She seemed terrified. What could I do?"

"Call the police?"

"She begged me not to."

He frowned, his eyebrows almost meeting, his eyes dark. "I told some guy out there to get lost."

"He's the one. We were both in here, listening."

He made an annoyed sound, and I knew he thought I should have let him know about Amber last night. But if I had, I knew he would've tried to persuade me to kick her out. I changed the subject.

"What do you think's going on, Percy? Why did she leave?"

He drew open the velvet drapes in the office and examined the tiny, dripping-wet garden.

"What was she wearing?" he asked.

"Last night?" I thought. "A very tight skirt, nylons, high heels, and a too-small waist jacket. Why?"

"I get that she could unlock the back door and go outside, but how did she leave? Think she could climb?"

I peered over his shoulder, trying to imagine large Amber clambering up the rain-slick brick walls that enclosed the garden. "Pretty much impossible," I had to admit, "even if she took off her heels."

"Fire escape?" he suggested, looking up at it.

"She would have had to climb up the old wisteria and pull herself up."

"I think she'd be too heavy. The wisteria's delicate."

We gazed upward—there was no sign of anyone on the fire escape.

The rain was taking a respite, and Percy went outside in the garden, staring up at the brittle wisteria branches. They were delicate all year round, even when laden with the most gorgeous fragrant bunches of violet-blue, but now, in March, they still looked seriously fragile.

I watched him for a moment, admiring his muscular bare arms and broad back, then went upstairs to the second floor opened the window. "See any footprints?" I called down to him.

"Too wet. The ground's soaked." He gently shook the trunk of the wisteria. "Should I try climbing it? See if I can?"

I would have liked to watch him do that, but when I looked at the branches near where they met the fire escape, I hesitated. The fire inspector had recently ordered me to cut the wisteria back, and Percy had done a thorough job on it. Now it looked particularly stark. I examined where the vines twined around the fire escape and saw no sign of anyone climbing up it. No broken twigs—nothing.

"Better not," I said. "It's too delicate. And there's no way she could have hoisted herself up it to reach the fire escape. She must weigh over two hundred pounds."

He came back inside and came up the stairs to the second floor where I was. It was just one large room and a bathroom. The front of the house looked out over Gay Street and the kitchen area was near the back, the window framed with the wisteria.

Percy hoisted himself on the sill, and examined the branches from the outside, searching for broken twigs.

"How'd she get out, then? No way she could've climbed those walls."

We looked at each other.

"I don't like it, Percy. I really don't. Are there signs of digging out back? Was she murdered and buried in my back yard?" I was only half-joking. This didn't feel right at all.

"You're sure you bolted the door when you went up to bed?" he asked.

"I know I did. I was nervous about the man on the stoop, remember? Besides, they were bolted this morning. I saw you sliding them open."

Agitated, he came back inside, went over to the front window and looked out. "I don't get it."

"Anyway, she's long gone."

Percy was very suspicious. "Why'd she come here? When did you let her in?"

"I didn't. She took the key that was in the basket when she left yesterday. You know I always leave it there for emergencies. She let herself in. She was here when I came back from Judy's."

We both went over to look in the basket. There was a pair of my taupe suede gloves and some silver coins for the supermarket, which I don't like to carry with me unless that's where I'm going.

No key to the house, though.

"Uh-oh. Looks like she still has it."

Percy was furious—mostly with himself for not being more vigilant about the front door key. "What the hell? Why would she do that? I'm calling a locksmith right away—we're changing the lock this morning! Otherwise she can just wander in and out whenever she wants! It's outrageous."

"I know. That would be great if you could take care of that."

"Anything else?" He roved restlessly around the room and I tried to think of a task that would keep him busy.

"Yes, can you find out more about the Thistle Gallery? If that man on our stoop was the owner, I'm curious to find out more."

"Shouldn't we tell Detective Cleveland what happened?"

"Let's wait. If you look at it, nothing actually did happen. Cleveland's not going to be interested."

"What happened was a total stranger lay in wait for you in the middle of the night and demanded you tell him where one of your clients was. You found same client hiding inside your house, and she claimed the man on the stoop was going to kill her. She then disappeared before you were awake in the morning."

"I know."

"She might already be dead, as far as we know."

"I'll try to track her down."

"How?"

"First I'll go to the gallery. If she's not there, well, you have her address, right?"

He nodded, reluctantly. Getting contact information was part of Percy's intake before I saw a client. He said we wanted to send a card to every client at the end of the year. He also sent all my clients e-thank-yous, and then after several weeks he snail-mailed reminders that they might be due for another consult.

"It's really just to thank them for their business," he'd said when he'd first started working for me. "Do you know that lousy customer service is 90 percent of the reason why people leave a business? We're going to make sure that not more than 10 percent of your clients are ever unsatisfied with our customer service."

I sometimes think Percy should give business

seminars.

But now he regarded me uneasily. "Why not send me?"

"Because you're still preparing for our meeting with the tax accountant. You said yourself you're way behind. And our meeting's later this week."

"I'll stay late."

I smiled. "I don't want you to stay late. I want you to have a life."

"This is my life."

"I'm not going to do anything rash," I said, laughing. "I promise I won't be lured into a dark alley. I'm just going to see if she's okay."

He went back downstairs, and about half an hour later I took my cloak off its peg by the front door and slipped out while he was on the phone, trying to get a W2 from some place that was remiss.

Within a few minutes I was on the A train to Dumbo.

 Exiting at Cadman Plaza West, I headed toward the overpass and continued on Old Fulton Street. As I walked down the hill I could see the Manhattan Bridge looming like a huge misty smile through low clouds.

I turned on Front Street, and found my way to the dark orange brick building with the three Scottish landscapes in the window. My velvet-lined hood fell back as I looked up, but it was drizzling again, so I pushed open the glass door and went inside. Maybe I was going way beyond the call of duty for a mere client. Percy would say so. But Amber was more than that. She had begged me to let her spend the night in my house, saying she was afraid of being murdered.

Then she disappeared.

I needed to know that she was okay.

The front foyer opened into the large, airy reception area. More landscapes hung on the white walls. There was no one sitting at the desk near the entrance, so I wandered toward the back. A door with a sign that said "Employees Only" was right behind it, so I figured that's where everyone was, although I couldn't hear any voices.

"Hello?" I called out.

The door shot open and a slim woman with cropped mousey hair and bright blue eye shadow came out immediately, a cell phone in her hand. She closed the door firmly behind her. "May I help you?"

"I'm looking for Amber Witherspoon."

She jerked as though I'd given her a shock, and then gave an anxious glance at the closed door behind her.

"She's not here."

She was so obviously lying that I laughed. "Come on."

"She's not! I swear."

She was acting so scared that I was tempted to step around the desk and open the door to see for myself. Instead I said firmly,

"Amber stayed at my house last night and left something that I need to give her."

"You can leave it with me." She stared with

hostility at me, as though she half-expected me to draw a dagger from the gold lining of my cloak. "Who *are* you?"

"Satyana. Who are you?"

She looked blank when I said my name, but answered, "I'm Kathleen, the office manager. Leave whatever it is with me, and I'll see Amber gets it."

"Oh, so she is here?"

"No."

Exasperated, I stepped around her and thrust open the door that said *Employees Only*. I looked around.

Empty.

It was more of a storage room than an office. There were no windows, no other exits. One wall was lined with shelves filled with office supplies: boxes of pens, legal pads, a postal scale, file folders. In front of the other wall was a large desk with paint tubes, brushes, and a canvas that looked as though it was being restored. Beside the door was a coat rack with a wet raincoat hanging on it, and a silvery vinyl tote bag beneath it.

Amber's?

I stepped inside. There was an unwrapped sandwich on top of a small table in the middle of the room. Beside it was a notepad that had random-looking numbers written on it. The bright green logo at the top said "Lucky Investments."

"You're not allowed in there!" the woman shrieked, grabbing the door handle from me and almost shoving me back into the reception area. Furiously, she slammed the door behind us.

I looked at her, puzzled. So she wasn't lying after all: there was definitely no one inside. But then why did she keep looking over her shoulder, as though someone was in that room? It made no sense.

Lucky Investments.

I thought hard and fast. Percy had said the gallery owner and this receptionist had won the lottery more than a typical number of times. Was the gallery a front for a lottery con of some sort?

"Okay," I said mildly. "Maybe you can help me, since Amber isn't here."

"I'll try." Her blue eyes were cold and wary.

"You all have a lottery pool going, right? I wondered if I could get in on it, even though I'm not employed here. I am a customer, though."

She looked even more cautious. "If you want to get involved you'll have to talk to Robert McNeil. He's in charge."

"Is he here?"

"No, he'll be back later this afternoon."

I took a blind swing. "I gather you all pool your money together to buy lottery tickets each week. Are you part of that?"

She gave a quick nod, eyes curious and cold. There was something so drab about her, the grey sweater and black baggy skirt, that she almost seemed invisible, except for her sharp eyes.

"How many of you work here?"

"Three," she said.

"Who are the others?"

"And all of you paid for lottery tickets? You do this every week?"

She looked at me strangely, as though she wasn't quite sure what to make of me. "Yes."

"Can you tell me how it works? Do you all pitch in and take turns buying the tickets or do you all go to the store to get the tickets together?"

She looked at me with a stare that unnerved me. Her eyes were so opaque I wondered how she could see out of them. But her response seemed normal. "No, we all give our share to Robert. He's the boss." Frost settled on her, making her seem pale as winter. "Look, if you're interested in talking with him yourself, he'll be back later this afternoon."

"Where does he buy the tickets?"

"Some place near his house."

"How often?"

She cooled even more. "Look, you need to talk to the boss about this."

"Okay, I will. Please ask Amber to call me when she comes back. She has my number."

Outside I changed my mind about trying to track Amber down at her apartment. It was a long subway ride out to where she lived, and chances were I'd ring and ring the doorbell and no one would answer.

The wind had picked up and I shivered.

Even though I felt that my intuitive powers had been suspended for over a year, I *knew* something was wrong.

 When I got back home, Percy jumped up from behind his desk and came over to help me remove my cloak and hang it on the coat rack by the door. "Any luck?" he asked.

"Not exactly." I smiled at him, grateful for his youthful energy and chivalry. He'd told me a while back that his parents had named him Percival after the questing, lovelorn knight of King Arthur's round table, and he'd always hated his name. But sometimes when he looked at me a certain way I felt it suited him. "I met the office manager though. And I need you to find out about something: Lucky Investments. Heard of it?"

He was back at his desk within seconds.

"Bring your laptop upstairs," I invited him. "I need to make myself some tea. Want some?"

"No, thanks." He grabbed his laptop and followed me. "By the way, the locksmith will be here this afternoon. I figured it was worth paying for rush service."

"Yes, I agree."

In the kitchen area, I filled the electric kettle and then sat down across from him at the small dining table while he did some exploration on his computer. Eventually, he looked up. "So. Lucky Investments. It's a new firm, just two years old. They don't invest in very much, they're not public."

"Then what are they about?"

"They purchase lottery tickets for people."

"As investments?" I asked doubtfully.

"Looks like it." His eyes gleamed mischievously. "You see? I knew there was a way to beat the system. Wonder how they do it?"

"That's so weird. Does anyone believe you can 'invest' in lottery tickets?"

He smiled too, but more grimly. "I guess some people still do."

I retracted, remembering his fascination with the lottery. "I mean, you buy lottery tickets, but you're counting on luck, right? You're not 'investing', are you?"

"No, not investing." He went back to his screen.

"But what?" I prompted him.

"Looks like they only buy tickets for the Cloverleaf Lottery. It's relatively small. It caps at two million dollars, and if someone hasn't won, the money's distributed between the next closest winning numbers. You have to pick 4 numbers out of 100 to win the two mil." He did a quick calculation. "That means odds are about 10,000 to one you might win even a small something."

I longed to say something sarcastic about the fools who buy into those odds, but refrained.

"Each ticket costs $4. It's got a four-leaf clover theme, see? But you have to buy a minimum of ten tickets. So everyone shells out $40, at least, just to be part of the game."

I shook my head. "That's just crazy."

"You might think that the idea that anyone could win—ever—is even crazier. But they do."

"They do?"

"Yes, and some people win more than others. Over and over."

I waited, intrigued.

"Specifically, investors in Lucky Investments win."

"So how do you think that works? Is there a way of cheating?"

"In order to win the Cloverleaf Lotto, you have to pick the correct 4 numbers from 100 possible balls. The order in which the numbers are picked is not important; you just have to pick the correct 4 numbers."

"Right."

"At first, the odds of picking a single correct number depend on how many balls have been chosen already. For instance, let's say none of the 4 numbers had been picked yet and you had to guess just one number correctly. Since there are 100 numbers to choose from, and since 4 balls are going to be picked, you have 4 tries at picking the number correctly. The odds of picking one number correctly are 100/4 = 25:1."

"Aha." I tried to follow intelligently.

The kettle was about to boil and I examined my tins. I went for Moroccan mint, since it felt like a good midday tea, and then, realizing it was past noon, I brought out some carrots, cauliflower and hummus for us to snack on. The peppermint aroma filled the room, but because the tea was mixed with gunpowder green tea, it had a slightly vegetal scent as well. It was one of my favorite daytime teas, but Percy wrinkled his nose and opted for plain water.

"Then there are the odds of picking another number correctly after one number has already been drawn. We know there are 99 balls left, and that 3 more balls will be drawn. So the odds of picking a number correctly after one has been drawn are 99/3 = 33:1. Now let's say 3 numbers have been picked and you have to guess what the last number is going to be. There are only 97 balls left to choose from, but you only get one shot at it, so your odds are only 97:1."

I was getting lost here, but I nodded.

"So that way we can calculate the odds of picking the right number when two or three balls have been drawn. You know the odds of a coin toss resulting in heads are 1/2 = 2:1. The odds of two consecutive tosses both resulting in heads are 1/2 x 1/2 = 4:1. The odds of three consecutive tosses all resulting in heads are 1/2 x 1/2 x 1/2 = 8:1. The odds of picking all 4 lottery numbers are calculated the same way—by multiplying together the odds of each independent event. The Cloverleaf added one ball to the game last week, so people had to pick from 101 balls, and the odds increase to about 4 million to one."

Have I mentioned Percy is a mathematical genius? It was something I discovered fairly recently, although I recognized his technical genius from the moment we met.

"I still don't get it." The three minutes' brewing time was up so I removed the metal filter from the teapot and poured myself a cup.

"When a lottery is capped at $2 million, and no one wins, the money is filtered down to those with the next most chosen numbers. Remember, I told you that before."

Yes, I remembered now. "So there's the likelihood of more winners. Makes sense. But I still don't get Lucky Investments. Is it a scam, do you think?"

"Seems so, although could be semi-legal, in some way."

"And I wonder what role Amber had in it—if any."

Percy frowned, his mouth full of bread and hummus. "Do you think she might have won big time? And then didn't know what to do with the ticket? I mean, she didn't want to share it with anyone else?"

"Percy! That's brilliant! I bet that's exactly what happened!"

 I half-regretted that I had agreed to go with my friend Brigitte to hear Avery sing at a nightclub later that night. For one thing, Avery didn't usually go on stage till eleven or sometimes even later, and between her sets she liked to sit with us and chat, which meant I wouldn't be getting home till the wee hours.

But I hadn't seen my two good friends nearly as often as I used to, now that business was going so well, and I missed them. Brigitte was an interior designer, who gave me (or 'loaned', as I preferred to call it) the fabulous Ward Bennett furniture, which had transformed my foyer and office.

Avery was a singer-songwriter who worked as a

paralegal by day but was getting popular by night, playing all over the city and New Jersey. In the summer she was mostly out at the Hamptons, playing in clubs there. She had a great, jazzy, low-key, sultry voice, played piano like nobody's business, and wrote some lush songs, too, which she interspersed with some old-fashioned romantic favorites.

Percy had closed up his part of the office and left — he'd said he had plans for the evening.

The rain had stopped earlier. The temperature had plummeted and the March wind bayed like a pack of coyotes. I dressed warmly in a long knit skirt, faux-fur-lined boots, and sapphire blue silk and cashmere on top. My gloves were silk-lined, and fit snugly, so I wouldn't have to take them off in the club, unless we ordered food.

Wrapping my cloak around me, I ventured out and immediately got hit by the yowling wind. Usually Gay Street was sheltered from those wild streaks of bitter cold that hurtled down the avenues, but this one found its way right to my doorstep. I hurried to Sixth Avenue to grab a cab, tussling with the wind for possession of my cloak.

Twenty minutes later, I was at the club on 85th Street near Lexington and warming up with an adequate sparkling rosé and Brigitte's radiant smile. She'd brought a man along: Ian. He had reddish-gold hair, greying around the ears, and a craggy jaw and a rugged, dimpled chin that made one want to kiss it. He was adorable and I felt almost envious of Brigitte. How did she manage to land such great-looking men?

"Ian's visiting us from Scotland," Brigitte told me

in her faint Texan drawl. "He's a poet."

"Och, aye, well, I try to be." Ian's eyes twinkled at me as though he'd known me a long time.

That another Scottish man had unexpectedly shown up in my life took me by surprise, but he was so darling I tried to ignore the too-obvious coincidence. He flirted charmingly with me and I was quickly smitten.

To my surprise, Brigitte, who was the most vivacious flirt I'd ever known, wasn't all over him, as she usually was on a date. She was dressed stylishly, as usual, in a fire engine red stretchy mini-dress, red fishnet stockings, and satin high heels with two rows of tiny buttons down each side. How she managed to keep them so pristine in the slushy weather was amazing.

Avery joined us for a few minutes before her set started. I wondered whether Ian would flirt with her as much as with me, but it was clear that I was the one he was interested in. We chatted all together, then she went back onstage and Brigitte went to the restroom.

Ian was looking at me with an expression I couldn't read. "So you're a psychic," he said. "What's that like?"

"What do you mean?"

"Do you get flashes of the future?" He seemed genuinely interested. "Or is it more of a feeling…how does it work?"

"It's more of a feeling," I smiled back at him. "An intuition." No reason to tell him my intuitive powers had deserted me and I was mostly floundering around with just my wits and my past experience to help me.

"Fascinating."

"What do you do? Besides write poetry, I mean."

"Just poetry," he said. "It's my life."

For some reason, I felt like he was lying, but I like poetry and I adored his Scottish accent, so I let it pass. I had to remind myself sharply that he was Brigitte's date, not mine.

"Where can I read something you wrote?"

"I'll recite for you." He broke into charming, and totally incomprehensible, Gaelic.

I smiled. "You have such a way with words."

"Thank you."

"Where did you meet Brigitte?"

As though I had invited him to, he drew his chair close to mine so that our thighs were touching. "Oh, through a mutual friend. We actually hadn't met before tonight."

He was looking at me with candid interest. His eyelids lowered slightly, as though we had some sort of understanding. It didn't take an intuitive to recognize the expression.

But he was Brigitte's date. I shifted my chair away.

"How long have *you* known Brigitte?" he asked, leaning toward me.

"Forever," I said. Meaning, *she's my friend, and I'm loyal.* Don't hit on me.

His eyes were deep midnight blue, like I imagined a highland loch would be.

"For some reason I thought you'd be older than you are," he murmured, still leaning toward me. "I had a different image of a fortune-teller."

"Really?"

"Yes, a little old lady with a shawl... but you're breathtakingly beautiful."

I smiled modestly. "I'm fifty."

"Ha."

"It's true. Well, almost."

He laughed, then nudged over his chair so that our thighs were touching again. I gave him a look that warned him to lay off the flirting.

"So, where did you meet Brigitte?" I asked again, wishing she'd come back from the restroom.

"I told you, through a friend." He leaned closer, and his voice lowered. "She's not my date, darling, so relax. Actually, I asked her to bring me here—I wanted to meet you. Didn't she tell you?"

"No. Why did you want to meet me?"

"We have a mutual friend, lass. Amber Witherspoon."

 Okay, in spite of being attracted to him, I now felt curious. How did Ian know about my slight connection with Amber and why would he want to meet me?

"You know who I mean?" he asked.

I didn't respond. I went on staring at the stage, where Avery was singing "Cuddle up a Little Closer" in her jazzy, lustrous style, and remembering how scared Amber had been the night before, hiding in my office.

He leaned close again and lowered his voice. "Amber's a friend." His Scottish accent now sounded clipped and cold. "She told me she went to see you. A friend of Amber's is a friend of mine."

"She's not my friend," I corrected him. "She came to see me for a consultation. Just business."

"Then I'd like to consult with you, too."

"Call my assistant." I tried to make my voice light. "He'll set you up with an appointment."

"I was hoping you'd read my cards for me here, tonight." He smiled at me, but it looked more like a dog snarling.

"The office is closed for now. But do tell me how you know Amber?"

"Mutual friends. We met at a party."

"Okay—and?"

He smiled affably. "Can I buy you another drink?"

"Sure, thanks."

He ordered a Coke for himself, and another sparkling rosé for me. I decided to probe a little. First the guy on the stoop, and now this handsome Scotsman.

"And why did you want to meet me, just because we both know her?"

"Did you hear she's disappeared?"

I wasn't sure how to respond. "Has she?"

"You know she has. You saw her last night, didn't you?"

Had Amber told Ian she'd stayed the night in my house? Could he have been the one who'd let her out? And then he'd climbed up the wisteria to the fire escape?

"Why do you think so?"

"She told me."

"Well, then, evidently she hasn't disappeared."

"Ah, but she has."

"Well, if you're hoping I know where she is, I'm going to disappoint you. I have no idea."

"That is very disappointing." He sipped his Coke.

"Do you live here? Or in Scotland?"

"Och, sadly I'm returning to dear old Edinburgh next week. But it's been a grand visit."

Brigitte returned at last, with fresh ruby-red lips and darkly smudged eyelids. Avery took her break and we ordered a chocolate mousse to share. Avery, it turned out, really liked Ian—or at least maybe she sensed my coolness and was trying to make up for it by being extra-nice to him.

"Tell us about your poetry," she asked him.

He immediately broke into another recitation, but since the whole thing was in Gaelic again I couldn't assess his talent. The other ladies gazed at him, enthralled.

When he'd regaled us with a couple of these, Avery returned to the piano and I said I had to leave. Brigitte said she was leaving, too. So of course Ian said he'd go with us. Then I felt bad about Avery, since it would be awkward if an entire table left just as she was about to start a set.

"Actually, I'm going to listen to a few more songs," I said.

"Me too," said Brigitte. They both sat back down.

Ian bought us another round of drinks, including another Coke for himself. I noticed he hadn't had any alcohol all night. We didn't need more dessert, but we looked at the menu again and considered the options before turning them all down.

We ended up staying for the entire set and leaving with Avery afterward. I was very sleepy.

"Where are you staying?" I asked Ian.

"A friend's apartment. Upper West Side. Where do you live?"

"The Village."

"Pity we can't share a cab then." He whistled shrilly, and a cab swerved over and screeched to a stop. Avery, Brigitte, and I piled in. He shut the door and lifted his hand in a wave.

The cab set off.

"So what was that about?" Brigitte demanded. "Why were you so cold to him?"

"He said he asked you to introduce us. Why? How did he know about me?"

"He didn't say."

"Three days ago a woman came in for a consultation," I told my friends. "The next night, I found her hiding in my office. She seemed frightened. I let her stay over, but she left before I woke up. I've tried to track her down, but no one can locate her. She hasn't been at her regular workplace."

"What does she have to do with Ian?"

"He wanted to know where she was."

They were puzzled.

"What do you think?" asked Avery.

"Amber was scared when she was hiding in my house. I know that for sure."

"Scared of what?"

"She said it was a man who was waiting for me on my stoop...you can see why this Ian guy made me nervous. He definitely wanted to find out whether I knew where Amber is."

"Hey, sorry I fell for him saying he wanted to meet you," Brigitte said, not sounding sorry at all. "But how exciting!"

Brigitte's apartment was closest, so she got out first, handing me some bills for her share of the ride. Avery was next, and I was last. The cab pulled up in front of 22 Gay Street. I paid the driver and emerged onto the curb.

The cab drove off. It was quieter now—the wind had died down. It was past two in the morning, and no one was around. The light was out in Percy's apartment.

I noticed something, though, in the well of his entrance. It looked like—someone was lying there.

A bum, passed out from too much booze?

I saw a leg, a plump feminine leg, wearing stockings and blue high heels with little sparkling jewels on them.

Definitely not a bum, not in this cold, not with those high heels.

I leaned over the rail. The woman's face was in shadow, but her body was twisted from the fall, and I could see her eyes were staring and lifeless.

Amber Witherspoon.

 "Percy!" I hammered on the window between the bars. There was no response. The gate was locked, but since it was just four feet high I climbed over it easily and kneeled down beside Amber. I put my hand gingerly on her wrist. It was warm, so I grew hopeful.

"Amber?"

She didn't move. I tried to help her sit up, and that was when I saw the blood gushing from a wound somewhere in her body.

Her lifeless eyes stared at me, and I knew she was dead. But only just.

Faint with shock, I fished out my cell phone from my cloak pocket and dialed 911.

"There's someone lying outside my building!" I said, as calmly as I could. "I think she may be dead, but you'd better get an ambulance here fast."

I gave the dispatcher the address, then debated what to do. I longed to go inside and bolt my door, but of course I felt obligated to stand vigil. I could use some rescue remedy, so I did leave her for a few minutes and dashed to my shelf of flower essences. On my way back, I grabbed the fleece throw that was on the couch in my office, the same one Amber had used when she'd spent the night. It just felt too weird and cold to leave her lying out there without being covered.

I leaned over the rail again but decided not to use it after all. The police would want to find things exactly as they had been when I discovered her body. I draped the throw over the rail instead and waited tensely.

Sirens were screaming by this time, and a police car pulled up in front of my house. Officer Blesson, who already knew me, made sure she really was dead by pressing his middle finger against the side of her throat. Then he spoke into his phone, requesting an ambulance to take the body to the morgue for an autopsy.

"Recognize her?" Officer Blesson asked me, shining his flashlight on the corpse's face.

I nodded. "Yes. She came to me a couple of days ago for a consultation."

"One of those psychic consults?" he asked. His expression was serious and impassive, but I'd witnessed his kindness from an interaction we'd had earlier that year.

The other officer wrote something down while Blesson went to speak to the ambulance driver, who'd just arrived. He asked for my name and phone number, then said, "What kind of consultation did you say, ma'am?"

"Psychic reading," I told him. "We had an hour-long session, and then she left." I didn't add that she'd come back later and spent the night inside my house. It just seemed too complicated.

I couldn't think straight.

Where was Percy? He must've heard the commotion. Other people were hanging out their windows, wondering what was going on. My neighbors from across the street, Ted and Lucy, came outside in their dressing gowns and I told them what happened.

"A bum?" Lucy asked. Lucy was a sweetheart of a neighbor, one of my favorites on Gay Street. His real name was Lucius, but he preferred Lucy.

"Doubt it, dressed like that," replied the officer. "Recognize her?"

He shone the flashlight into her staring eyes again. Lucy and Ted shook their heads, looking upset.

"How did she die?" someone else asked.

Another officer had taken some flash photographs.

"Not sure, but looks like a stabbing."

"Look around for a knife," ordered the police officer with the notebook. He held up the fleece throw I'd left draped over the rail. "Whose?"

"Mine. I thought I'd cover her, but changed my mind."

He looked suspiciously at it, then at me. "I'll take it with me, if you don't mind."

I did mind, but there was no point in arguing. They'd find a hair or bit of old skin on the throw, accuse me of withholding evidence, and I'd repeat the fact that she'd been in my office just three days ago.

In any case, it would take repeated washings to remove the energy of the dead lady from it. Maybe they would do me the courtesy of a nice dry-cleaning before they returned it.

Not likely, though.

The EMT crew zipped up the body bag, and shoved the gurney into the back of the ambulance. It took off, but no sirens this time.

It was almost four o'clock in the morning.

"I'm sure Detective Cleveland will call you in the morning," Officer Blesson said.

"I'm sure he will."

I went inside, still wondering about Percy's absence. Maybe he was staying over at a friend's house. Maybe even a girlfriend he hadn't told me about. We tended to avoid talking much about his private life.

I closed and bolted the door, still shaky, then hung up my cloak, removed my gloves, and left them in the basket where the front door key had been.

I was very glad Percy had changed the locks on both the front and back doors. I had one set of new keys, and he had the other.

And the third, spare set was safely locked in his desk drawer.

Detective Cleveland was an old friend. Well, not exactly a friend. We'd had our differences when he was trying to solve a case in which he thought I'd been peripherally involved. He didn't trust me at the beginning, but as things wore on, he began to respect me more.

He was a large man, with grey chunks of eyebrows that seemed to stick out farther than his nose, which was not small. His eyes were dark and restless, but when they settled on me with a direct question sometimes even I felt the need to fidget.

And now here we were again, with another body

on our hands. We were sitting in the front room, Percy behind his desk, and me on the windowsill of the bay window overlooking Gay Street. It wasn't eight o'clock yet, and I'd slept very little even when I did finally crawl into bed. I could tell Percy was kicking himself for not being here last night. Apparently, he'd stayed over at a "friend's" apartment. He didn't elaborate.

I told Cleveland what little I knew about the victim, including the fact that the night before last, she'd let herself into my office and spent the night.

"She'd taken my spare key. But she left before Percy or I were up. Neither of us saw her leave."

"Hope you changed the locks." Cleveland glared at Percy.

"Yep," said Percy.

I also told Detective Cleveland about the man who'd been waiting for me on my stoop, demanding to know where the murder victim was, and that she'd seemed afraid of him.

"Afraid how?" Cleveland demanded.

"She said she was afraid he'd kill her."

"Humph. Hm. Description?"

"He wore a baseball cap, so half his face was in shadow. Thin… it was hard to see." I hesitated, then decided to tell him: "But he seemed genuinely concerned about Amber. I don't see *him* as a murderer."

I paused again.

Cleveland's chin jerked up and his eyebrows jutted out alarmingly. "Go on," he demanded.

"I met someone else last night who was trying to

find her. He'd asked my friend Brigitte to introduce us—we met at a bar. His name's Ian something. I can find out his last name. Brigitte might know. But I don't trust him. Definitely something shady about him."

Cleveland focused on his phone for a moment, tapping things into it. Then he cleared his throat and looked up. "What name did you say? 'Ian'?"

"That's right."

"Hm. We'll follow up—no need to ask your friend. We can do that. And there's nothing else you can tell me about this Amber person, eh?"

I scrunched my brow, trying to remember. "Not that I can think of," I said at last.

Cleveland put away his oversized cell phone, where he wrote all his notes, and said goodbye. I watched through the bay window as he got inside the squad car and drove off.

I turned to Percy. "When's my first client?"

"Ten o'clock. An hour. Cancel it?"

"No, I'm okay." I could tell there was something nimportant he wanted to tell me. "Can it wait? I need to clear the air before I meet with anyone."

He looked annoyed. "I didn't say anything."

"I know." I tried to cajole him with a smile. "But can it wait?"

He stared pointedly at his screen, his fingers tapping the keys. I could tell he was itching to ask me something, or tell me something, or talk about what had happened. But I needed a moment. I closed my eyes, briefly, overwhelmed by sadness that I hadn't been able to save Amber from her fate. Now all I could do was help the police find her murderer.

I thought about Ian again. There was definitely something he'd been concealing from me. And if Amber had been waiting on my stoop for me, Ian could easily have gotten to Gay Street by taking the subway, way before I'd arrived in the taxi.

And had plenty of time to stab her to death.

Well, *maybe*. I'd have to check that out. We'd left the club at two in the morning, dropped off Brigitte, and then Avery. How long did that trip take?

And how long would a subway take, if it had arrived within, say, ten minutes of Ian reaching the station?

I just couldn't rule out the fact that he might have murdered Amber.

"Ahem."

My eyes flew open. A stranger had entered so quietly that we hadn't even heard the front door close.

Even Percy looked startled, but he recovered almost immediately. "Hi, do you have an appointment?"

I recognized the intruder at once. It was Kathleen, the opaque-eyed, mousey office manager I'd met yesterday. She was still mousey. Rain had soaked her gray jacket and she must've forgotten her umbrella. Her hair was thin and sticky.

It was strange the way she looked at me. I couldn't get a read from her. Usually, unless I'm consciously putting up a psychic sort of armor around me, I absorb what people are like, whether I want to or not. When an intruder enters my home, I naturally want to get some sort of read. Not anything weird. Just the same sort of thing anyone would do. Is the intruder friendly? Dangerous? Hostile? What do they want from me? What do they seek?

But in this case I sensed — *nothing*.

 She looked at Percy and nodded impassively at me, her pale face bland. Her hair was ashy and short under a grey wool beanie. Her nose was sharp and red. "I just heard about Amber. I was at work."

"Yes, it's so sad."

She looked around.

"Percy," I said. "This is Kathleen. I met her at the office where Amber worked."

Nodding shortly, Percy waited for a sign from me regarding how I wanted him to deal with the visitor. And, frankly, I wasn't sure. I didn't have a sense of mistrust, nor a sense that I needed to learn something from her. But then why was she here? Did she need my help?

I gave Percy no signal and so he stayed where he was. Kathleen moved to the open door of my office and I instinctively followed her, waiting for her to tell me why she was there. She seemed uncomfortable, as though she wasn't expecting me not to invite her in to sit down.

"Where did she die?" she asked.

"Outside, on the stoop."

I thought she would find the place, maybe proffer a flower or photo. But instead she went on looking around the room. Her eyes rested on McCoy Brown's painting on the wall, and then on the mantel and the low oak chest between the sofa and my throne chair.

"Do you know what happened to her?" Kathleen asked, her eyes wandering to the thick drapes drawn back from the tall windows. "Who murdered her, I mean?"

"No, not yet." I looked at her stiff back. "Do you?"

She turned and eyed me, as though I'd offended her.

"Why did she come to you in the first place? And why would a person want to kill her right outside your house?"

"I don't know."

"You must know. Why here? Why last night?"

Okay, I'd had enough. Percy was standing in the doorway, waiting. I nodded to him and he cleared his throat.

"Sati, you have a client soon. Kathleen, if you'd like to make an appointment to see Sati you need to speak to me."

I tried to look apologetic and resigned, as though my schedule was out of my control, and that I regretted having to turn her away.

At the same time, I didn't want to lose a connection to Kathleen. Maybe there was something she knew. I had to find out why Amber had died.

"If there's anything you'd like to tell me before you leave, please go ahead. Do you have any idea who killed her?"

"No." She lowered her eyes so she wasn't looking at me. Lying? I still couldn't tell. "But did you find her cell phone?"

I frowned. *That* was an interesting question. Most people carried a cell phone with them, but I didn't remember Cleveland mentioning one.

"Why?"

"It had details about the purchase of a painting. A client is claiming one price, but it's not the price we have listed. Without her phone and the details she has there, I can't move forward with the sale."

"Why doesn't your client forward the texts to you?"

"He refuses. And my boss is breathing down my neck."

"Have you asked the homicide detective at the police station for the phone?"

"Yes, of course. He said there wasn't one. But everyone has one. You found the body. You might have taken it."

I smiled, but barely. I was definitely intrigued now, and finally starting to get a read on her. She wanted Amber's missing cell phone, and she wanted it badly.

"I'm sorry. I don't have it."

By this time Percy had managed to edge her out of my office. At his desk he asked for her contact information, politely soothing her with promises of getting in touch with her if we found out anything about Amber's cell phone. I stayed in my office, but when I heard the front door close, I went back out.

"What was that all about?"

He put his finger to his lips, and gestured to the window with his head. I glanced out. Kathleen was pushing open the gate to his basement apartment and stepping into the well where I'd found Amber's body. We both went over to the window, gazing down at her in surprise.

"Do you think Amber's cell phone fell out somehow and the cops didn't find it?" I said.

He nodded.

"I'd rather find it myself." I felt edgy. "Can we ask her to leave?"

"No need," Percy pointed out. "She's leaving now."

We quickly ducked out of sight, in case she looked up and saw us both staring at her.

"Uh-oh. Do you think she found it?"

"Nope."

We watched her push open the gates and without a backward glance head toward Waverly Place.

I felt myself breathe more regularly. "How can you be sure?"

Percy looked bland, but I could tell he was containing his excitement. "'Cause I have it. That's what I wanted to tell you. I found it this morning when I came home. Lodged under the gated part of my door. The cops couldn't have found it without unlocking my door. It fell at my feet. And I took it inside."

 He took it out of his shirt pocket and handed it to me. It was an iPhone with a pink hard case. I let it rest for a moment in my hand, then turned it over a couple of times. I looked up at

him.

"Locked?"

"Yep."

"Why didn't you tell me you had it?" I tried to sound stern but I was too excited.

"You—" he began.

"I know, I'm sorry. But why didn't you tell the detective?"

"I wanted to try to unlock it first. I've tried just about everything. Birthdate, her address."

I held the phone in my hand, trying to think of a way to get into it. Percy had charged it using his own charger, but it most definitely was locked.

"Detective Cleveland would be able to figure out her passcode," I pointed out.

"Should we ask him?"

"We probably need to tell him we have the phone, yes," Percy said. "Otherwise we're withholding evidence. I meant to when he was here, but I wanted to show it to you first."

I turned the phone over again, longing to know its contents. Percy watched me.

"What if there's something on the phone that would help us figure out who murdered her? You're the intuitive. Maybe you can piece together something that he can't."

"Even if Cleveland doesn't suspect me of murder, I don't think he trusts my intuitive powers enough to have me look at numbers on a cell phone. I think we just have to hand it over."

"What if there isn't a client who bought a painting through Amber? What if there's something else she wants to find on the phone?"

"Like the winning lottery numbers? Or, if she had a winning ticket, where she might've hidden it?"

"Maybe."

"Can you find out whether there's a winning lottery ticket that's been claimed yet?"

"Think the murderer has something to do with that?"

"Two million dollars *might* be a motive. Could Amber have won, and Robert found out?"

"She double-crossed him so he killed her?" he sounded doubtful. "Seems too much of a coincidence. But what should we do about the phone?"

"Can you find out about her parents?" I asked. "She said she lived with them up till a couple of years ago."

"Sure. Cleveland will be there ahead of us, though."

"That's okay, let him do his thing. I just want some background, a landscape to place her in. She seems such an enigma, even though she came to consult with me. I want to know more about her. She did mention that her parents were under financial strain. If she won the lottery it might have changed her life."

"Want me to call Brigitte and get more info about your Ian friend?"

"She'll still be asleep. Better wait." I hopped off the windowsill. "I'd better get ready for my ten o'clock. Who is it?"

"Miriam Smith. Another recommendation from Ruby."

I hurried upstairs for tea and some toast. I wanted

to do a little clearing of the ruffled energy in my office before I began. I needed to infuse calm, clarity, and peace into my space.

There was something about the energy of a dead body outside one's building that required extra diligence.

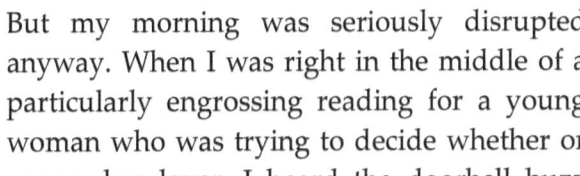 But my morning was seriously disrupted anyway. When I was right in the middle of a particularly engrossing reading for a young woman who was trying to decide whether or not to marry her lover, I heard the doorbell buzz insistently and then a loud pounding on the front door. It was ridiculous, since the door was kept unlocked during the day, when Percy was sitting right there at the reception desk. I tried to ignore it, knowing Percy would deal with whoever it was.

I heard the front door slam, and then my office door was flung wide open. Standing there was Robert McNiel, Amber's elusive boss.

I saw Percy's enraged expression behind him. His eyes asked me whether I wanted him to punch the intruder or politely show him out.

I was not sure myself. But then I saw his red, distressed eyes, and my heart melted. This man was seriously grieving.

I summoned my Voice. "You need to wait your turn," I said, calmly and sternly. "Sit in the chair in the waiting room and I'll meet with you when I'm ready."

My voice was not loud, but had an emphasis that

made it almost impossible for someone to resist doing what I said.

While Robert hesitated, Percy spun him around, piloted him to one of the scissor chairs in the waiting area, and thrust his index finger into Robert's chest so that he fell into it. Then he shoved a *New Yorker* into his hand.

"Read," he ordered.

Even though Percy didn't know how to use the Voice like I do, Robert opened the *New Yorker* and stared blankly at a page.

My client, thankfully, realized that this was probably not the best time to make a decision about her future, especially not one as grave as marriage.

I apologized for the intrusion, but she took it very well. I got the sense that she liked the drama, which boded well for the future, because whatever happened with regard to her marital status, it was certainly going to involve massive amounts of melodrama. I gave her some meditative practices to do while she got to the heart of why she was unsure about which step to take, and I advised her to come back next Monday. "I won't charge you for the follow-up," I told her, even though I knew Percy would object. "Do these exercises in the interim. That way you'll come to your decision with a lot more clarity."

We went out to the reception area together, and she rescheduled her appointment with Percy.

I went over to Robert.

"All right, come on in," I said. "I have half an hour, and that's it." I made sure Percy heard me say that, so he would be ready with his ringing of the bell.

We went inside my office and I sat in my burnt orange chair across from him. He was on the couch, feet hard on the floor, hunched over in a posture of despair. He dug his elbows into his thighs, buried his face in his hands, and burst into heaving sobs.

I stayed quiet, letting him cry, and when he calmed a little, I handed him the box of tissues that was always nearby. Eventually, he took one and blew his nose loudly.

"I can't believe she's gone," he choked. His voice was faint.

"I know," I murmured soothingly.

"I mean—she was just here—so alive—"

I was sympathetically silent.

"I knew it—I *knew* it," he blew again. "I can't believe this is happening!"

"How did you find out?" I asked.

"She didn't call, she didn't show up—she just disappeared. Then this morning the police came to the office, wanting to question us. We're all in shock."

"I'm so sorry."

He was growing more aware of his surroundings. "This is where she was?" He looked sadly out the window and then at the McCoy painting over the mantel. Then he turned back to me. "You saw her here, right? She told me she was going to come and see you."

I nodded.

"Did she say anything about me? Did you talk about me at all?"

I knew he didn't need me to respond—he was grieving and just wanted to talk about the dead woman he had loved. He went on gazing around the room, as though Amber might be lurking somewhere there. His longing for her felt authentic. Maybe he really had been smitten.

The singing bowl hummed through the closed door. Our time was up.

"I'm sorry, Robert, but I have another client coming. I wish I could help you. If there were any details you'd like to have about how she died, get in touch with Detective Cleveland. He'll tell you whatever it is you need to know."

He burst into tears again.

 After he'd gone, I stared at the couch, puzzling and wondering. Just because Amber had been found dead on my doorstep, it didn't mean I was responsible in any way.

But I *felt* responsible. She'd spent the night in my house, on that very couch, and then the next night she'd died on my stoop.

I felt as though her death had something to do with me, and I couldn't shake the feeling. If only I'd come home just a few minutes earlier. Or if I hadn't gone out at all... had she been ringing and ringing my doorbell, hoping to get to safety?

I wished with all my heart that I'd been able to prevent her murder.

Percy stood in the door, waiting for me to look up. When I did, he asked, "What did he want?"

"I'm not sure. He was definitely upset. Seems like

he really liked her."

"An act?"

"Maybe. Did you find out anything?"

"Amber's parents are retired. They've lived in the same house since they were married. She moved out a few years ago."

"I can't get it out of my head that her murder had something to do with the lottery."

"Maybe."

"But it's so unlikely she won. I don't know what she was hinting at when she came to see me, but I can't believe that she was really seeking advice on what to do because she'd won two million dollars. She'd go see a lawyer."

"If she was smart."

"I wonder whether there's something else."

"Like what?"

"Something else entirely..." I closed my eyes, trying to see more clearly. "Maybe this murder has nothing to do with that."

"I did a little digging around on the woman who came here earlier. Kathleen Jones."

"Oh?"

"Raised in a military family. Moved around a lot, mostly in the States. Got into trouble, sent to juvie for a while. Living in Florida at the time. Seems like a tough girl."

Percy and I were both hungry by this time so we went upstairs and I heated up a carrot soup I'd made over the weekend. Percy sliced a baguette and smeared the crusts with goat cheese. I made us a pot of green tea.

As we ate, the spring wind rattled the windows and I was glad to be inside. The pink phone lay between us, on the table. We kept looking at it.

"Well, what did you feel?" Percy asked, his mouth full. "When Kathleen was downstairs, I mean. Didn't you get a sense of who she was?"

"No—nothing."

He quirked a dark eyebrow in surprise. "Nothing?"

"And nothing will come of nothing…" I felt very low. "I think this time my intuitive powers really have gone for good, Percy. It was such a weird feeling not to experience any sense of what kind of person she was, who she was – just… *nothing*."

Percy regarded me sympathetically.

I shrugged off the gloom. Early spring did that to me sometimes. I poured myself a second cup of tea and picked up Amber's phone again.

"It's an iPhone 5s," I said, half to myself.

"Right."

"What if she locked it using her fingerprint? "

"Could be…" he conceded. "But she'd have used *her* fingerprint."

"I know."

We looked at each other.

Then Percy shook his head. "Her body's probably still in the morgue."

"Well, then, when's the funeral?"

He checked his phone. "Day after tomorrow. At a funeral home in Queens. Looks like there'll be a mass, too."

I was getting excited. "So her body will be moved

there, maybe tomorrow? For embalming?"

Our eyes met, and Percy's widened in disbelief as he read my mind.

You've got to be kidding me," Percy said softly. "You can't sneak into a funeral home, find her body, press her fingertip to a cell phone, and hope it unlocks!"

"Why not?" I asked.

 He exploded. "For one thing, I'm sure it's illegal. For another, it won't work."

"Is it possible, though?" The idea was exciting me. "I mean, she'll have been dead for two days. Would her fingerprint still work—would the phone recognize the print?"

He shook his head. "Sorry, but no. Only a finger attached to a beating heart will be able to unlock it."

"But why? Isn't it just a visual scanner?"

"Not exactly. It needs to be alive—that it, it needs to have an electrical charge to activate the scanner, not just the image. The tissue has to be living."

I nodded but asked, "How does it work?"

"The sensor?" He eyed me curiously. "It's capacitive, so there'd have to be liquid still in her finger. Basically, it reads pores, ridges, valleys and also senses an electrical charge from living tissue nerves. Then makes an identification."

"How would I do it?"

He shook his head, not meeting my eyes. "You'd place her finger on the sensor. It'll look at the fingerprint pattern on the conductive sub-dermis layer of skin located underneath the dermis layer. But I'm telling you, it won't work if she's not alive."

For some reason I didn't believe him. "Does the print have to be a certain angle? She might be pretty stiff."

"It recognizes fingerprints oriented in any direction."

"So if her hand or arm is at a funny angle it could still work."

"Yep." Percy shrugged and looked away. "But it won't work."

I nodded. "I heard you."

"And anyway, how would you get permission to see her body? You're not a police officer or a detective, or even family."

"True. And if Cleveland found out, he'd hit the roof."

"Might even arrest you for tampering with the evidence. We need to tell him we have the phone."

"Yes, of course. Let's wait just a little longer. I want to think."

He didn't look happy but I went upstairs, mulling. There was something Percy wasn't telling me, I was sure of it.

There had to be a way to unlock that phone.

In the living-room area I stood by the window overlooking Gay Street, my own phone in my hand, trying to decide whether or not to call Leandros and get his advice. I compromised by texting:

Looking for some funeral home fun?

 Leandros was one of my oldest friends. We've known each other since middle school, and were crazily in love for several years between then and now. Eventually, our paths separated, and now he was happily married and living in Los Angeles. But we were still friends — and it was not romantic *at all.*

He had his own extraordinarily successful law firm, but he was always on the lookout for adventure.

He called me right back instead of texting.

"Hey, you."

"Hey," I said, smiling just at the sound of his voice.

"Tell me about it."

"A client was murdered last night, right outside my house. It was awful. Then this morning Percy found her cell phone — the cops had overlooked it. We're trying to unlock it before handing it over, hoping there's a clue on it that could help us solve the mystery of who killed her. We might be able to unlock it with her fingerprint."

Leandros chuckled. "Want me to go to a funeral home, find her corpse, squish her dead finger against the sensor, and hope the phone will unlock?"

"Think it could work?"

"Might. Companies claim there's no way, but enterprising people keep showing otherwise. But you're withholding evidence. Why not give the phone to the cops and let them figure it out?"

"Because Cleveland's not going to tell me what he

finds out. Why would he? And I might be able to piece something together. I think Amber was involved in something…maybe big."

"Aha. What did she consult you about?"

"She said she wanted to know about a guy she liked. But now I think there was something else."

"Like what?"

"I just wonder if her death had anything to do with me. I could tell something was wrong when I read for her. Maybe I could've prevented it." I swallowed. "The night before last she was hiding in my office. Said she was afraid her boss would kill her. She ended up staying over." I told him about the man on my stoop and about Ian, who'd wanted Brigitte to set me up on that date, and by that time I'd confused even Leandros so much—and he tends to be one of the most clear-headed people I know—that he said he'd better get on a plane and come and check things out for himself.

"But I'm tied up till Friday night, unfortunately," he added. "I'll take the red-eye and be in New York Saturday morning. Is there a wake?"

It always amazed me that with a schedule so busy, an office so successful, and a family life so vibrant, Leandros could hop on a plane to New York at a moment's notice like that, but so it was.

"I think they're doing the autopsy today. She was stabbed, so it was definitely murder. If there is a wake, I'm guessing they'll take the body to the funeral home afterward to get it prepped. The funeral's Saturday afternoon."

"That'll be too late. You'll have to sneak into the

funeral home and unlock the phone yourself."

"But how? Percy says there's no way I can use her dead finger to unlock the phone. It has to have live tissue."

"That's just what the company wants you to believe. People have shown over and over that all the sensor actually does is read the fingerprint. They call it a 'deep skin' fingerprint but that's just jargon. And I'm sure your Percy knows it—he probably just doesn't want you to get into trouble."

I grew hopeful. "So all I have to do is press her dead finger to the phone and it'll unlock?"

"I didn't say that. It may be more complicated. Her finger may be so shriveled the sensor can't read it."

"So how would I do it?"

"You could try by taking a super high-res photo of her fingerprint, clean it up, invert it, laser print it onto transparent sheet with a thick toner setting. Then you'll need to create some sort of fake skin. Wood glue might work. Let it dry. Then pull it up, breathe on it so it's moist—the sensor needs moisture to work—and try it."

I was mad at Percy for not telling me about this option. "So all I really need to do is sneak into the funeral home and take a photo of her fingerprints."

"Might work. No guarantees."

 When I'd hung up I had another bright idea. Brigitte had recently purchased a new-fangled beauty product that she'd wanted me to try— a non-surgical facelift gadget that she'd recently purchased. She'd been encouraging me to borrow it so I could see its wondrous effect for myself. What it did, according to her, was to stimulate reactions within and between the cells of your skin by using tiny electrical impulses. "Your skin will be rehydrated, your circulation improves, your whole face is firmer and smooth," she'd urged me. I'd always preferred the idea of aging gracefully, without any kind of external procedures, so I'd declined in spite of the significant glow I saw in her face. But now I thought I might borrow it and see if it might work more easily than making some sort of complicated copy of Amber's fingerprint.

I went downstairs. Percy was seated behind the desk, working on the computer, a pile of receipts beside him. He glanced up.

"Your next client's not till four," he remarked.

"I know. Percy, when's Amber's funeral?"

He tapped some keys. "Saturday at two pm. There's a wake on Friday. My guess: they'll do the autopsy today and embalming tomorrow."

I went to look over his shoulder. "What are the hours for the wake?"

"Seven to nine p.m." He looked curious. "Why? Are you going to it?"

I said something vague, and left him to his tax receipts. I texted Brigitte and asked to borrow the device she'd offered and then, since I had a few hours before my next client, I decided I might as well use the time to determine whether Ian had the opportunity to get to my stoop and murder Amber before our cab arrived. I walked along 8th Street to Astor Place and took an express to 86th Street. The club where Avery had sung so sultrily a few nights before was closed up, the padlocked gate a dull silvery sheen.

When I got to the place where Ian had bundled us into a taxi, I pressed the stopwatch on my phone and sprinted to the subway. It roared in almost right away, which, I had to admit, was unlikely in the middle of the night. I waited for the next one, but even that one came in way sooner than I figured it would at two a.m.

I hopped on, clocked the ride, then sprinted along 8th Street toward Gay Street. Seventeen minutes.

My cell phone buzzed. Detective Cleveland. I answered.

"We checked out your throw, Ms. Satyana." He only called me by my full name when he was cross with me. From the beginning it had annoyed him that I only had one name—same for first and last. "How come it's got hair from the deceased on it?"

"Does it?" I tried to remember. "Oh, right. Well, she came for a consultation, remember? I already told you about that."

There was a silence and I realized someone must have told him she'd stayed the night in my office. Who, though? Who knew she'd been there? More importantly, who let her out the front door, bolted it, and escaped up the fire escape?

"Oh, and she came back the next night," I added quickly. "She'd stolen my key. She felt threatened."

"So that's the key we found on her." He heaved an annoyed sigh.

"Yes."

He harrumphed. "You're not telling me everything."

"I told you she was scared," I said. "There was a man on my stoop and she said she felt threatened by him. It was Robert. But I don't know if she was telling the truth or not. Honestly, that's all I know."

He harrumphed again.

"Have you tracked down that other man I told you about—Ian?" I asked. "The more I think about his strange behavior, the more I think he knows something about Amber's murder. And he knew she'd spent the night at my house. He said she'd told him."

This time he sounded even more annoyed with me. "We'll deal with any suspects. Stay out of it. And next time tell us the whole story, not just the parts you feel like sharing."

 On Friday evening, the day of Amber's wake, a cold, windy rain rattled the windows. I was deeply immersed in a knotty knitting problem in a cardigan I was working on, and did not relish heading out in that at all.

Still, Amber's fingerprint awaited me. I was so

curious about what might be revealed by unlocking her phone that I didn't reconsider going out, in spite of my coziness. Dressed in a sage green, close-fitting, jersey knit dress and tartan-patterned tights, I pulled on my high leather boots, which were pretty enough to wear indoors, but also serviceable in a light rain. I took my cloak off the hook by the front door, tucked Amber's phone and Brigitte's device—which she'd been delighted to loan me—into the pocket lining, and ventured onto the damp, windswept street.

The light in Percy's basement apartment was on, but he'd drawn the curtains. Briefly I considered inviting him to come. He'd want to, I knew. But he was my employee, my assistant, and he did way too much for me already.

I would do this on my own.

The funeral home was in Queens, so I jumped on the E train. Although my consulting business was much busier than it had been, taking a taxi all that distance was out of the question.

I emerged at the nearest subway station, walked the four blocks, and then circled the building a couple of times before going inside, just in case. If I did manage to remain hidden inside the building after the wake was over, I might need a different escape exit than the front door.

The doors of the funeral home were wide open and Amber's wake was already in progress. I was greeted by a pudgy young man in a gloomy suit, and the usual somber, sympathetic expression that comes with a job at a funeral home.

"My condolences, please come this way," he said

automatically.

"Good evening," I murmured, drawing close enough so the jasmine behind my ears might waft to him.

His mournful expression brightened and he looked me up and down.

I quickly saw he could be an ally.

He immediately offered to leave his post and take my cloak to the cloakroom. I kindly refused, my gloved hand lightly resting on Amber's phone, snug in the inside pocket.

"Crowded in there?" I asked, taking out a mint from my clutch and offering him one.

"Not very," he said, taking the mint as though it was a precious gold coin. His voice was surprisingly high. "Are you friend or family?"

"Friend. Well, sort of. I was like her—therapist."

He looked impressed. A taxi pulled up and a man and a woman got out. They looked grim and sad, but the man noticed me, and I think he liked my cloak because he gave me an up-and-down look before following the woman inside.

When my new friend had ushered them respectfully inside he came back to stand next to me. I smiled.

"They didn't even say hello to you. Is that how most people act at a funeral home?"

"Oh, I'm used to it. I don't take it personally anymore."

"Of course not." The building had three stories, and all the lights were out on the top two floors. Was there a cellar? "Have you worked here a long time?"

His lips curled up proudly. "I own it."

That startled me. "Really?" He couldn't be much older than Percy. "Congratulations. Must be a lucrative business."

"This place belonged to my grandfather and my father...he died last year. Left it to me." He held out his hand and I shook it. "Peter Dashwood. Yes, we make money. People just seem to go on dying."

Our eyes met in humorous mutual understanding, and I thought that beneath the relentless pretense of sympathy for the bereaved, he was a nice guy.

"I'm Satyana."

"That's a lovely name. And it suits you."

"Have you always been located here?"

"Since 1945."

"You do the embalming here too?"

"Absolutely. We have the best facilities in the city."

"Are you an embalmer?"

"Used to be, but now I manage the business. But in a pinch I'll help out, or if I want to try my hand at a new technique. There are always new chemicals being introduced that I'm interested in."

"What happens to her body after the wake is over?"

"We'll take good care of her remains," he reassured me.

"I mean, does she stay in the room? Or do you move her?"

He looked at me curiously, and I realized how odd my question must sound. "What I meant was," I added hastily, "is she going to be buried or cremated?"

"Buried. Tomorrow, after the funeral."

"Do you keep her body here until then?"

"Yes, ma'am." His voice became super-reassuring again. "She'll be well-attended. One of our directors always accompanies the body to the church. Everything is done very respectfully."

"Oh, I'm sure that's true. So after the wake, you move her body into another room? Tonight, I mean?"

"Yes." He seemed a bit disconcerted by my directness. "Everything is handled very respectfully, I assure you."

"I guess I should go inside," I said, making my voice sound reluctant. "Is it an open casket?"

He nodded. "But she looks real pretty, I assure you."

I realized there was nothing more to be gained from him, at least for the time being. I needed to look around inside, and somehow figure out which room Amber's body would be taken once the wake was over.

The front hall was empty. Several shiny side-tables were topped with boxes of tissue that sprung up like frosted cupcakes. My heels sank into the lush carpet—dark blue with a brown pattern underlying it.

My nose twitched. Air freshener, lilies, and... something else I couldn't place.

Voices came from the large room around a corner. I paused by the guest book, but didn't sign it. I'd rather not have a permanent record of my presence there, just in case... well, I wasn't sure what might happen, but whatever it was, I knew I did not need to include my name in that book.

I peeked into the room. It wasn't large. The coffin was lay on the far side, surprisingly well lit. I'd come near the end of visiting hours, so the receiving line had already dispersed. Instead, small groups of people stood by the side of the wall and several people sat in rows in the seats facing the coffin.

To my startled surprise, I recognized Ian seated in one of them.

 Our eyes met, and he proffered a chilly nod, entirely unsurprised to see me there. Too startled to react, instead I approached the coffin to pay my respects to Amber's corpse. Peter Dashwood had been right: they *had* done a nice job on her. She looked lovely. Dead, but lovely.

I didn't pay much attention to her face, though. I was looking at her hands, folded peacefully on her solar plexus, and wondering how on earth I was going to get Amber's fingerprint to open the iPhone. Would my scheme work? Did they embalm fingertips, and would injecting fluid into them affect the prints?

I didn't even know which finger she might have used for a passcode, which meant I might have to try all ten of them. How long would that take?

I realized I was spending too long at the coffin, and turned away. I may as well find out why Ian was there.

There was an empty seat next to him, and I took it.

"Nice to see you again, lass," he said in a clipped

tone.

I smiled at him. He looked very different than he had in his jeans and sweater of two nights ago—this time he wore a dark suit, white shirt, and a gray tie. His red-gold curls were neatly combed, and his strong craggy jaw with the delicious dimple in the chin was closely shaved.

"It's so awful," I murmured.

"Indeed it is." He stared straight ahead.

"I don't think you told me how you knew Amber?" I asked.

"I did tell you. We have mutual friends."

"Are they here too?"

"No."

"I found her, you know. Soon after we said goodnight."

"So I heard."

I stared at his profile.

"I didn't kill her, lass," he said, glancing sideways at me. "Did *you*?"

I went on looking at him, too deep in thought to answer. Who was Ian, really? Why had he persuaded Brigitte to introduce us? He'd said it was because of Amber—but why?

Just because I'd had a consultation with her?

Very suspicious.

Still, he was so damned attractive.

"Can I take you out for a drink after you've paid your respects?" he inquired.

I was tempted, but I had a job to do and I didn't want him hanging around waiting for me after the wake. "Maybe some other time."

He looked disappointed. I wondered if he really did like me a little, or whether he was after something else.

"Tomorrow, then?" he asked.

"Yes, maybe that would work."

"And I'd really like to get that consultation you offered."

"Give my office a call," I said, flashing him another smile. I stood up. Maybe it would be best to find a hiding place now and wait till the funeral home had closed, or else I might find it hard to shake him.

I left the main room and walked along the hall. A couple was kissing in a small anteroom and I hastily backed out. Halfway up a flight of stairs a small group was gathered, talking, sharing a small flask.

There were just too many people around.

I went into the ladies' room, and realized I wouldn't be able to hide in here. Peter Dashwood would no doubt make sure no one was left behind before locking up, and the room only had one stall, which made it easy to check.

My heart sank. Maybe this just wasn't going to work. But the thought of Leandros's laughing eyes incited me. I longed to be able to tell him I'd been successful.

Just then I heard a strangled cry of grief and headed quickly toward the sound. Robert staggered out of the main room where the coffin was and practically fell into my arms.

Gently, I put my hand out and said his name. "Come with me," I said, using my Voice. "Let's get you a glass of water."

He buried his face in my shoulder as I supported him out of the room, murmuring soothing words of encouragement. Some people were watching us, but they didn't look surprised by his grief. It was a funeral home, after all.

I found a chair in the hall and sat him down, shoved a box of tissues beside him, and went to ask the cloakroom lady for a glass of water. She complied immediately, and within seconds of my returning to Robert's side, she was there with a tall glass of ice water.

"Drink this," I ordered him.

Valiantly, he tried to, choked, then, at my urging, he tried again. Finally he calmed down enough to ask, "What're you doing here?"

"Same as you. Paying my respects."

He choked, drank more water. "I can't believe she's gone."

He looked as though he might start wailing again so, to forestall him, I asked him about Amber's phone.

"The police haven't been able to find it," I said. "You don't happen to know where it is, do you?"

He shook his head, his eyes watery and dull. He really did seem upset.

"I just wondered if maybe there might be a clue on it. Like who she was planning to see that night. Did she meet someone? Phone number?"

He shook his head again. Evidently, Amber's murderer was not as important to him as the very real melancholy he felt at her passing.

I felt sorry for him. We sat together for a while, while he calmed down, and then he told me he felt better, but that he wasn't going to stick around any longer.

"There's no point. Shouldn't have come here. Going home."

"That's a good idea. Get some rest, Robert. You look like you haven't slept in days."

"I haven't," he admitted, his eyes watering again. "It's so hard—every time I start drifting off I jerk back and start crying."

I gave him a small bottle of a flower remedy, telling him to put a few drops in water or under his tongue when that happened.

"'Rescue remedy'," he read out loud. "You're rescuing me?"

"Try it," I smiled encouragingly at him. "You'll see."

He thanked me, hugged me tightly as though I was his best friend in the world and he could hardly bear to say goodbye, then went out the front door.

 I debated my next move. It was already past nine o'clock and when I poked my head out of the room where I'd taken Robert. I saw several guests were lining up at the cloakroom to get their raincoats. A closed door on the other side of the small room lured me to it. I pushed down the gleaming brass handle and the door opened into an unlit hall.

I had no idea what I was doing, and hoped Cleveland—if he ever found out—wouldn't be *too*

angry with me. I also hoped that Ian had long since left. Quickly, I closed the door behind me and stood in the dark. The sound of my breathing felt strangely loud. Was I really planning to remain in a deserted funeral home after everyone else had gone?

I felt my way along the hall until I came to some carpeted stairs. Back here I heard no voices, no sounds, not even the lively traffic from the city streets outside. It was as though I was in the very heart of the funeral home, deep in the center of the house of the dead.

At the top of the stairs I felt my way along a hallway that led to another closed door. Since there was no sound, I turned the handle to this door and entered.

It was very cold in here. The smell was intense— mostly a cinnamonish aroma, but not the kind people might sprinkle in their coffee. I waited while my eyes tried to get used to the dark, but it was, well, too dark. Nothing happened, even after a few minutes. The room stayed dark.

I took out my phone and used the flashlight. Pointing it around, I saw I was in a large room that had no windows. Storage units lined every wall, metal containers that looked like giant file cabinets.

They didn't store files in them, though. I could tell from the smell.

I did not want to stay in here. I was chilled through, despite my warm cloak, which would probably have to be dry-cleaned now. The smell was intense.

But it did seem like a good place to wait. I

crouched behind a table, out of sight in case someone came in. If they decided to search for me, I'd have to come up with some explanation.

Maybe I'd pretend I was temporarily insane.

I didn't dare turn on the light, in case someone walked past in the hall and saw the sliver of light underneath. I wondered what Peter Dashwood would do with Amber's coffin when everyone had left downstairs. Would it be wheeled into another room? Would it be left where it was, the top down? I hoped I'd be able to find it.

I settled myself more comfortably, resting my head against the thick, soft hood of the cloak and wrapping it snugly around my body. I still felt cold, but I was getting used to it.

An hour passed, and then another. I was getting used to the smell, which I supposed was both a good and a bad thing.

When I saw on my phone that midnight had finally rolled around, I decided it was probably safe to venture back downstairs and find Amber's body. I still didn't turn on any lights, and instead felt my way along the hall. When I reached the carpeted stairs, my gloved fingers slid down the banister.

The room where Amber's body had been was now empty. There was a little light floating in from a curtained window on one side of the wall. The place where the coffin had been positioned was now bare. Even all the flowers were gone.

But where had they been taken?

I left, went past the ladies' room, and kept opening doors cautiously, wondering where they kept bodies in readiness for cremation. The hall was getting chillier, so I had a decided feeling I was getting somewhere.

And now the smell came rushing back, and I felt a strong sense of fear and dread… Amber? I pressed my gloved hand to my mouth, and breathed in some calm and quiet, closing off any energy that might belong to someone else. At times like this, I knew it was important to differentiate between an energy outside myself and something I might be experiencing for myself, as a warning.

This was definitely an energy outside myself, so I calmed down. Instead I focused on 'seeing' without using my physical eyes.

When I thought I must be all the way at the other side of the building, I found a room that had two rows of five closed coffins. I left the door open, because the energy was so intense I felt it needed an outlet.

I felt pretty sure that Amber was in one of the coffins. But which one?

I went over to the one closest to me, removed the glove from my left hand, and placed my palm on the lid, around where I thought the head was. I felt nothing, no energy, no response.

I moved to the one beside that. Still nothing.

But the third one felt strange. It was almost like a vibration. I hastily put my glove back on and tried to pry open the lid. It was heavy, and for a moment I worried it might have been nailed shut. But it wasn't. Using all my strength, I was able to push it up.

With my other hand, I managed to put on the flashlight from my phone and flash the light onto the face inside.

Yes, there she was. Lovely Amber.

I was getting a strange sense of urgency. I had to try to open that phone of hers, and I had to do it fast. But how could I prop the lid open while I tried to do that maneuver?

Was there some sort of stick? Feeling around, I found a metal hinge and pushed it until it gave a quiet 'click' and the top was securely propped open. At least I hoped it was.

I took Amber's phone and Brigitte's contraption from my cloak pocket and turned them both on. The face-lift one required some moisture for it to work most effectively, so I delicately used some saliva, then reached for one of her still hands, neatly crossed on her waist. The contraption made a very faint vibrating sound, and I massaged her left thumb with it awkwardly. Her fingers were stiff as nails, and as cold. It was hard to move them—I had to nudge it under her hand. The shock of feeling her cold, rigid flesh made me cringe. After a few seconds, I gently pressed it on the sensor.

Nothing happened with the phone.

I steeled myself to try again with her index finger.

And then I heard a faint noise in the dark room behind me.

I looked up, and almost fainted with fear.

The burly figure of a man stood in the open door.

Then he was coming ominously toward me.

I screamed.

 It was just a soft scream, but there was no help for it. Scream one must, if one thinks one is alone in a dark funeral home, and someone shows up just as you're playing around with the fingers of a corpse.

"Do shut up, darling," the man whispered.

I recognized the Scottish accent at once.

Ian.

I almost collapsed with relief, or terror—I wasn't sure which. He came up next to me, chuckling softly.

"Who'd you think it was?" he asked in a low voice.

"Not you," I choked out.

"Come on, I said I wanted to take you out afterward."

"And I said I was busy."

"Did you now?"

"Yes."

He was still smiling, but his expression became chillier. "So, tell me, did you find what you were looking for?"

"What do you mean?" I was pretty angry now that I realized he wasn't going to stab me or strangle me or something. At least, not right away.

"Something to do with Amber's body?"

My heart was beating so fast I had to catch my breath. Anger wrestled with my relief at realizing he wasn't going to harm me, and then I distracted myself by returning to the task at hand.

"Tell me." His voice was firm. "Believe it or not, I'm your friend, darling."

I didn't believe that, not at all, but there seemed no point in hiding what I was doing. "My assistant found Amber's phone and I thought maybe I'd be able to unlock it by pressing her dead fingerprint on the sensor. I'm trying to find out who killed her."

"Are you now?"

"Yes."

"And how do you think her phone might help you discover that, then?"

"Maybe a text? Check out her contact list? Emails?"

"Why not let the police do that?"

A reasonable question. I answered honestly: "I wanted to look first. I wanted to see the numbers—I thought maybe I'd get some sort of intuitive insight into their pattern or a psychic flash from one of them. Numbers have that effect on me sometimes."

He drew in his breath, sort of a reverse whistle sound, and then chuckled again. "You *are* amazing." He sounded wholly admiring.

"But her phone was locked, and I thought I might be able to unlock it with one of her fingerprints. It's not working, though."

"Of course not. Won't work if the hand's not alive. Everyone knows that."

"Well, I had this idea. I'm going to see if it works." I held up the Brigitte's gadget. "It presses electromagnetic current into the dermis. I thought maybe I could fool the sensor."

He blinked. I used a little more saliva and

massaged it into her other thumb, then turned on the machine and applied some pressure.

Then, quickly, I pressed Amber's cold thumb against the sensor. I was getting the feeling that this was a ridiculous idea... maybe the warmth of her fingers was required in addition to the print itself.

Aha.

"It worked!" I breathed.

Ian actually let out a gasp, and I realized he'd thought I was making it up. I was too excited to stay mad, however.

"Now what?" I said, staring at the lit-up phone in amazement.

He took it from me. "First, let's make sure the phone doesn't lock again. Have to change the settings. Hopefully her finger's still electrically charged...what is that thing you're using, anyway?"

"It belongs to Brigitte. She uses it to give herself facelifts."

He laughed out loud, then handed me the phone. "Here you go. Want to check it out here or go somewhere else?"

I quickly scanned the phone for messages. There were several, including some that had come through after she'd died.

Including a lot from Robert, and even a few from Ian.

I shivered, realizing that if Ian had murdered Amber, he wouldn't want me to see these messages.

"You'll want to write down these numbers and the contacts," he said, his head close to mine as I hastily flipped through the screens. "Let's go somewhere and do it together. I'm interested too."

I'll bet you are, I thought. He made me nervous. He'd obviously known her, and quite well, judging from the number of phone calls they'd exchanged.

Just why was he so interested in Amber Witherspoon?

"Why are you so interested in Amber?" I asked.

"I'm not—I'm more interested in you."

"In *me*? Why?"

"Hm." He smiled. "Well, for one thing, I find you very attractive. And I also think you're brilliant. I like both those things in a woman."

Maybe he did, but I was sure that wasn't the reason he'd waited around a funeral home to pounce on me after everyone else had left.

"Okay, maybe we should get out of here," I said, slipping the phone into my cloak pocket.

We made sure that Amber's hands and sleeves looked as though they'd been undisturbed.

"Is there a back door?" Ian asked.

"How would I know?"

"You seem to know your way around this place pretty well," he pointed out. "Used your intuition, now, did you?"

"Yes, as a matter of fact, I did."

For some strange reason, he'd taken my hand. And stranger still, I didn't really mind.

"Let's see if we can go out this way," he suggested.

We crept along the carpeted hallway, still holding hands, like truant school children.

"I'm pretty sure this opens onto the alley behind the building," I said. "I circled the building before I went inside."

"I figured you must've. Okay, let's see. Hope it's not alarmed."

I hadn't thought of that. "Uh-oh. What if it is?"

"We'll have to run for it. Ready?"

I was starting to feel elated, not nervous anymore. The way Ian had handed me the phone made him seem almost harmless. And his hand in mine was firm and strong. Nice.

The back door did have the emergency lock bar, and when we pushed it the clanging and banging was deafening. Clutching my cloak around me, I leapt after him down the shallow concrete stairs and we fled, still holding hands, along the empty alley to the main road.

"There's my cab," he shouted. He was laughing.

"Cab?" I gasped, out of breath.

"I asked the driver to wait."

He waved his free hand as though it were a wand, and a taxi appeared. We clambered in, and he gave the driver my address.

Snuggled safely in the backseat, I breathed more regularly for the first time since I'd entered the funeral home several hours earlier.

Which didn't make any sense. Why had Ian hung around, waiting for me?

And how did he know my address?

 During the drive home he put one arm around my shoulders and pulled me close. His aftershave was fresh and citrusy, and his eyes danced in merriment.

"Shall we look at the phone together now?" he asked, pleasantly.

I figured there was no point in refusing. He was broad-shouldered and muscular, and could easily wrench it from me and take off with it.

His loch-colored eyes were fixed on me as I took the phone from my cloak pocket. It was impossible to know what he was thinking, except I could've sworn he liked me. A lot.

Looking down, I scrolled and glanced at the series of text messages first.

"Robert's the one who's upset," I said, skimming. Ian's breath was warm on my cheek as he leaned close. "He keeps wanting her to call him. Why d'you suppose she didn't?"

There were several texts from Kathleen Jones, but they were from two days before Amber had died. And they were nothing more than cryptic "lols" and smiley faces.

"What about phone messages?" he asked. "Voicemails?"

"Don't see any." I thumbed through her contacts.

"I don't see any patterns or weirdo voodoo thing that you might get from looking at numbers," he said.

"Do you?"

I couldn't tell from his tone whether he was being sarcastic. "What do you mean?"

"You're familiar with numerology?"

"Yes."

"And you claim you're psychic. That's why you wanted to look at the phone. So, do those numbers mean anything to you?"

I shook my head. "They're mostly stored as names so it'll take me a while to find any sort of pattern, if that's what you mean." I wished I knew whether or not he was being sarcastic.

"How did you know that she was the one in that particular coffin?" he asked.

"Hmm?" I went on studying the list. I looked up and found him still staring at me.

"Well?"

"What?"

He repeated the question.

"I could sort of see her through the coffin," I answered, truthfully.

"How?"

"You're really interested?" I asked, curiously.

"Very."

"I used the palm of my hand. I was trained by my guru several years ago."

His eyes were very dark. Lights from the highway kept crossing shadows across his face.

"How does it work?"

"It's hard to explain. You have to understand that we're made up of vibration. Humans used to have an internal organ that could register much finer vibrations than we can now."

"Vibration… you mean as in a form of energy?" When he saw me hesitate, he urged me: "I'd really like to know."

"Well, this organ was like a third eye. As humans evolved through the millennia, only a remnant still remains, near the pineal gland."

"Are we talking science or mysticism?"

"Both. During our embryonic development, our only 'organ' was the one we could feel with. We could experience hot and cold, for instance. Then this primal organ became our first sense, touch. It spread through the nervous system and through the skin. Our second organ was our one 'eye,' which we used to see all non-solid matter, because that was all that existed, right? As the earth solidified, we developed two physical eyes to view the solid world, and then that second organ recessed, and its etheric sight spread all over our nervous system and has its seat in our solar plexus. My yogi told me that all our five senses are going to eventually spread all over our bodies in a similar way."

Ian went on looking at me, his eyes warm and curious. "So you really can see through walls, for instance?"

I still couldn't assess his tone. "In the same way that an animal can," I replied slowly. "A cat or dog knows instinctively if there's a wild animal outside, long before they can hear or smell them. They 'see' them."

"Instinct. Or smell."

"Seeing through walls is rooted in the same thing.

It's instinct made conscious. We bring willpower and control to the experience. It's pretty dormant now in most people. But with developing and training it's not all that hard to reawaken. It's the kind of training that was taken for granted in the olden days, by the priests and rulers of Mesopotamia and Egypt, for instance. The third eye is represented by a symbol on countless statues all over India, or by a peacock's feather in the case of a Chinese mandarin. If you can really get your third eye to function, you're in touch with the greater part of the physical world, all that part which is invisible to the physical eyesight."

"There's an invisible world?"

"Of course."

"Explain."

The topic was so interesting to me that it was hard not to throw myself into my response, even if he was asking only in order to prove to himself I was a nutcase. "Our world is divided into seven interpenetrating planes: solid, liquid, gaseous, and four kinds of ether. Our regular old eyes can register or 'see' vibrations of the first three. The third eye can see the vibrations of the four ethers."

"You'll have to explain 'ether' to me."

"Think of it as vibration. We're vibrating particles. Colors vibrate at different rates. Crystals and stones vibrate at different rates."

"Okay," he said quietly. "You can stop now. This is beyond me." And then he pressed his lips on mine and I felt a sweetness go through me. Maybe it was just because the adrenalin from the adventure was making me giddy, but I wanted the kissing to go on and on.

It was a long drive back into the city, but much too soon the taxi let us off in front of my house. I said a quick goodnight to Ian and hopped out. But he was beside me on the sidewalk before I'd taken the first step up to my front door and grabbed my hand.

"Are you going to tell Cleveland you found the phone?"

"Yes, first thing tomorrow."

For some reason he looked as though he didn't believe me, but then he pulled me toward him in another embrace. His arms certainly felt nice around me.

He waited by the curb until I was inside my front door, then he held up his hand in a wave and got back into the cab. I smiled back, then let the front door swing closed.

I knew the door locked automatically. I'd been locked out enough times myself to know for sure it was locked. But the creepiness of the funeral home, and holding the hand of a dead person made me feel extra vulnerable, so I firmly bolted the door as well.

The clock on the brick wall behind Percy's neatly kept desk said four-thirty. I was very tired, and I'd be a wreck tomorrow if I didn't get at least some sleep. But something drew me into the office.

 Amber wasn't there now. Of course she wasn't. And yet I felt compelled to stand there, in the middle of the dark room, as though waiting.

I took a few deep breaths.

Then I closed my eyes. It didn't make much difference; the room was dark either way.

Leaning against the side-table, I asked out loud, "Who murdered you, Amber? Tell me."

No eerie voice spoke in the gloom, there was no faint fragrance of violets, nor the crash of a vase falling to the ground, thrown by a poltergeist. I wasn't disappointed—I hadn't expected anything like that to happen. I was asking myself, more than any ghosts.

But I also felt that the key to what had happened to her was very near to where I stood. I tried to recall our conversation when she had first come in for a reading. I went over every sentence, every word.

Nothing.

The only thing that had seemed out of character was when she'd lost her temper near the end. She'd leapt to her feet, accusing me of being a fraud and giving her bad advice, and then she'd stormed out.

An odd response?

Maybe.

On the other hand, I'd had clients do that before.

In the dim pre-dawn light, I could make out the painting of the stone circle hanging over the mantel. I didn't feel drawn to it, as I usually was. I turned away, exhausted, and went upstairs. But in spite of being so tired, I showered, rinsing my hair several times so that the odd cinnamon odor was well and truly gone.

I awoke late, of course, and felt groggy and headachy. I showered again, made a strong black tea and took it downstairs with me, then unlocked phone tucked in my other hand.

Percy was already seated behind his desk. I went over and placed it in front of him. Its pink plastic shininess made a sharp click on the top of the desk and he started.

"Check it out," I told him. "It's unlocked."

"How'd you do it?" he asked.

I described my evening, omitting mention of the make-out session with Ian in the backseat of the cab. I'd already checked my phone for a text from him, but there was nothing. What a night! Although sneaking around in a funeral home might not seem like a wild night on the town, it kind of was.

For a Scottish poet, he certainly was adventurous. And a lot of fun.

I was thinking about him way too much.

Already Percy had plugged a cord into Amber's phone and was engrossed in downloading every little bit of information he could squeeze out of it and transferring it onto his computer. I watched him for a moment, silently thanking him all over again for showing up in my life.

I cleared my throat. "Call Detective Cleveland and

let him know you found the phone, okay? If I call he'll think I've been withholding evidence."

"Yep—good idea," he agreed. He frowned, examining his screen. "Kathleen Jones."

"She's the office manager at the gallery. The one who came yesterday to look for the phone."

"Yes—a lot of texts from her. No calls, though."

"I noticed that too."

"There are quite a number from Robert. Especially on that night she stayed here. But she doesn't respond. He got mad."

"Do you think he knew she was inside my house?"

"Hard to say. There's something he wants her to give him."

"The lottery ticket?"

"Maybe."

He frowned again, and I prompted him. "What?"

"You're mentioned too, Sati."

"Me?" I peered over his shoulder. "Where?"

"A text from Amber to Robert. *'Going to Sati's to get it.'* Get what?"

"Maybe the lottery ticket? Do you think she left it here? What day was that?"

"The day she died."

"That means Robert knew where she'd be."

There was a loud knock on the front door and then the insistent ringing of the doorbell. Percy went to open it.

Detective Cleveland barged through the front door and he looked *furious*.

 Percy realized at once what was going on. Conciliatorily, he went to his desk and handed him the pink phone. "We were just about to call you."

"*Sure* you were," Cleveland snarled.

He snatched the phone from Percy, then came right up to me and stooped close so that his enormous eyebrows practically touched my forehead. "Where's that ticket?"

I stepped back, confused. "Ticket?"

"Yes, *ticket*," Cleveland growled, glaring. "Give."

"I don't have a ticket."

"Sure you don't," he practically frothed with sarcasm. "*Sure* you don't."

"I don't know what you're talking about."

"You can't use it, you know."

As he glared, I guessed Ian must've told him I had the phone. I felt betrayed, even though I'd intended to pass the phone along to Cleveland anyway. But I'd told Ian that. Hadn't he trusted me?

Did Ian *want* to get me into trouble?

"I don't have any ticket," I said.

Cleveland's glare turned to a stare. "Where'd you find the phone?" he asked, slipping it into his pocket.

"It fell between the gate and my door," Percy said, trying to distract him from his anger at me.

Cleveland went on looking at me. "Tell me the truth."

"That is the truth," I said.

Percy came over to stand beside me, his arms folded. Cleveland glared at him, then at me. I could tell Ian had told him *everything*.

What a jerk.

"You obviously know what happened last night," I said frostily. "Why ask me?"

"I want to hear your side of the story."

"Percy found the phone, as he said. It was locked. We thought maybe we'd be able to unlock it if Amber had used her fingerprint as a passcode."

"Why'd you want to unlock it? What's it got to do with you? Don't you think the police are capable of doing their job? What about messing with fingerprints?"

"I thought maybe I'd get an intuition about the numbers in her contact list. I *can* be intuitive on occasion."

"How well did you know Amber Witherspoon, *really*?" he snapped.

"I told you, she came to me for a consultation. Then she came back the next night, and said she was afraid for her life. She hinted that it was Robert, her boss, who was threatening her. Why not ask him?"

"We did ask him. He has no idea why she'd be afraid of him. He was crazy about her."

"So he says. But where was he on the night she was killed?"

Cleveland frowned. "Robert McNeil? He has an alibi. A woman. She's confirmed he was with her."

"Who?"

I thought Cleveland wasn't going to tell me—why

would he? But then he said, "Kathleen Jones. She works at the gallery too. They were both there working late, and ended up staying the night."

"Then what about Ian? He told you about last night, right? Who is he? How does he know Amber? He keeps saying 'mutual friends.'" I turned away. "I bet he killed her."

"Bah," Cleveland turned on his heel and left. The door slammed shut behind him.

"How did he find out that we had the phone?" Percy wondered out loud

"Ian, of course. I can't believe him."

My phone buzzed: Leandros had arrived.

Free for lunch?

I texted back: *Yes.*

Meet at Rendezvous at 1:00. And wear black—let's go to the funeral afterward.

My first client was about to arrive, and I definitely needed to do a little clearing of the atmosphere, after the detective's harsh mood and my confusion about Ian. I lit a clump of burning sage and circled the room, and half-considered putting Leandros's painting back in its former place over the mantel. If he came over, it wouldn't be easy to explain why his painting had been replaced by this old rendering of an ancient stone circle by a little-known Scottish artist.

I didn't have the time just then, though. I had to focus on clearing the energy. I especially had to clear Ian from my psyche.

Because in spite of the fact he'd betrayed me to Detective Cleveland, last night he'd seemed so … well, *nice*.

 In general, I tried not to wear black unless engaged in some ritual that required a great deal of psychic protection. Today I wore peacock blue velvet leggings and a sea-green mohair tunic with a Japanese-style twisted collar low on my throat, which was strung with several strands of jade and pearls.

"You look like a sea urchin," Leandros teased when I took off my cloak.

I would've preferred him to say I reminded him of a mermaid.

Rendezvous was one of our favorite lunch bistros. It was hard to find upscale vegan restaurants in Manhattan. Rendezvous was one of the best. It's too pricey for me usually, but that doesn't matter to Leandros.

"So what happened?" he asked when our drinks— champagne for me, a single malt for him—had arrived.

"You mean last night?"

"Yes. Were you successful?"

I wondered whether he really thought I wouldn't do it. "Yes, I was."

His steam-gray eyes lit up in admiration. "Well, how about that." I loved it when he looked at me like that. "Tell me what happened."

I recounted my adventure in the funeral home, and as I started to dig in to the unexpected appearance of Ian, just as I had discovered Amber's coffin, his face darkened.

"Who is this guy?" he glowered, pretending to be jealous. Sometimes I don't know how his wife can stand him, but I figure she must know him pretty well by now. They've been married fifteen years, he has two teenage girls, and they seem like a happy family.

"He says he's a poet from Scotland," I said, "but then this morning Detective Cleveland showed up and he already knew about the phone. Ian's the only person who could've told him. Why would he do that?"

"Trying to get you into trouble?"

"Maybe, but again, why?"

"Covering his own ass 'cause he's involved in the murder? Could he have done it?"

"Possibly."

"Anything curious in the victim's texts?"

"There were a bunch from the office manager at the gallery. She's the one who came to my house, asking about Amber's cell phone. That kind of alerted me."

"What's she like?"

"Nothing."

"What do you mean?"

"I couldn't get any sort of read on her. She was so damn neutral, it was weird. She didn't seem angry, upset, worried—nothing."

"Not everyone is as emotional as you are."

Sometimes Leandros can be so annoying.

"I'm not talking about her emotional life. I'm talking about her attitude—her way of being. Oh, never mind."

Sensing my frustration, he changed the subject. "How's the tiny house? Go there a lot?"

A few months earlier someone I'd helped out had bought a piece of property for me in the Berkshires and then surprised me by building my dream tiny house right on the side of the mountain. It was designed so that it was protected from the north winds by the back of the mountain. The valley spread in front—a panoramic vista of forest, sky, and a ridgeline across the valley that looked like the back of a dragon.

None of my friends had seen it yet. Well, Percy had, but only once, when he'd driven me there to meet the enterprising young woman who'd designed and built it for me.

"Not often enough," I admitted. "It's kind of hard to get to. Also, it's been such a chilly spring, and it would take a while for the wood stove to kick in enough heat."

He knew that that wasn't the real reason. The real reason was that I didn't have a car. I could take the train to Keesaugh, and then a bus into Tahton, but then I'd need to pay for a local taxi and be stranded up at my house or rent a car. In spite of Percy's amazingness in turning my business around in just a few short months, renting a car was still out of the question.

"But I'm going to spend a week up there as soon as it gets warmer," I said quickly. "It's so restful and inspiring. I miss it."

"Am I ever going to get to see it?"

"Maybe. We'll see."

I doubted it, though. The tiny house wasn't a place to bring friends. It was a cabin in the woods, a retreat, a place of stillness and alone-ness. But I knew he'd be hurt if I told him 'no' directly, and besides who knew? Maybe one of these days I'd invite him.

We ordered mole tempeh fajitas and a delicious seitan au poivre with roasted garlic mashed turnips, and then shared the dishes, as we usually did.

While we ate, he glanced for the hundredth time at his phone. "I'm checking up on the autopsy," he apologized, picking up on my irritation again. "I have a friend who knows someone who said he could let me know what came of it."

"Okay. Anything?"

"Two stab wounds, one in the chest cavity and one in the stomach. Whoever did it used a street knife, maybe a Raven—it had a wharncliff grind and a crusher point. She must have died around two-thirty. When did you find her?"

"About then. I was at a club with Brigitte and Avery. If only I'd come home just a few minutes earlier… she was still bleeding when I showed up. She was still warm."

He saw my expression, put his phone away, and glanced at the glittering watch on his tanned wrist. Leandros was one of the few people I knew who still wore a wristwatch and I liked to tease him about it, since it was probably worth well over $20,000. He didn't wear any other jewelry, not even a wedding ring, so it was like a bauble for him, and I knew he enjoyed looking at it.

"Funeral's at two. You game?"

"Okay."

I wasn't looking forward to it—it seemed a waste to sit in a chilly stone building when it was such a pretty spring day outside, but it was nice being with Leandros, and I knew he was curious about meeting the players in this odd murder I'd become entangled in.

Also, it was better for me to put my mind to trying to figure out who murdered her than to kick myself for somehow failing to prevent her death.

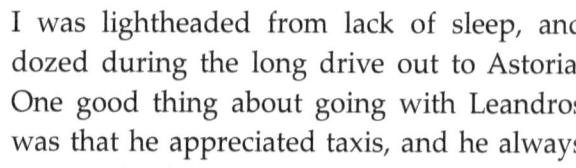 I was lightheaded from lack of sleep, and dozed during the long drive out to Astoria. One good thing about going with Leandros was that he appreciated taxis, and he always paid. He was glued again to his phone, sometimes texting but mostly talking into it with his strong, alpha-intense tone of voice that had so stirred me many years ago when we were young.

The funeral was at a medium-sized church across the street from where I'd been the night before. I felt more rested when we arrived and looked around curiously at the assortment of people who attended Amber's funeral. There were some somber twenty- and thirty-year-olds, clustered in groups—I figured they were friends from her school days. Robert was standing close beside an older couple whom I surmised were Amber's parents. The man's eyes were red-rimmed, but his face stoic and impassive. The woman was blanched with shock. Their grief was palpable, and as I murmured my condolences at the end of the interminable mass, I felt my heart heave over Amber's death again.

Could I have prevented it somehow?

I looked around surreptitiously, but didn't see Ian.

"Is the man you were with last night here? What's his name?" Leandros murmured.

I shook my head. "Ian? No, he's not here. I don't see anyone I know except for Robert McNeil, the head honcho at Thistle Gallery, and Kathleen Jones, his office manager. Why?"

"I'm thinking he must be the murderer." His mouth was close to my ear so no one else could hear. "Don't you think? Otherwise why would he be so interested in you—following you to the funeral home, and then sneaking up on you like that?"

"If he killed her, wouldn't he stay as far away from Cleveland as possible? And I'm sure he's the one who told him about my having Amber's phone."

"Not if he's trying to frame you."

"I had an alibi."

"Not really." Leandros pointed out. "You yourself said she still felt warm, so she must have been killed just minutes before you arrived on the scene."

"Maybe, but my bet's on Robert. She seemed so scared of him when I found her in my office that night."

Later, standing by the side of the grave, I watched Robert clutching a handkerchief to his mouth. He was trying to repress his sobs as he shoveled some dirt onto the coffin. Beside him stood Kathleen, staring straight ahead, her thin face cold and impassive, so stiff and motionless she looked a little like a cadaver herself.

 We didn't stay for the reception afterward— Leandros had been invited to some swish party in midtown and he wanted me to go with him. I realized only then that was the main reason he'd flown into New York for the weekend, not to see me.

"What's the occasion?" I asked.

"A fundraiser for something or other," he said, carelessly. "I told a friend of mine I'd drop in. You'll like her."

"I think I'm too tired. I only had a few hours' sleep last night. Who's your friend?"

"Clorinda Galmas. She's a bigwig in lots of organizations—always raising money for some charity. I've known her forever. Come with me. It'll be fun."

My cell phone buzzed—it was Percy.

"Hey," I answered it.

"Cleveland is back, this time with a couple of officers. He has a search warrant and they're snooping around. I had to let him in or he would've broken down the door."

"Know what he's looking for?"

"A lottery ticket."

"I guess he saw that text too. Did they go upstairs?"

"They're there now."

"Ugh."

"I'll tidy up when they go."

"That's okay. I'll be back soon, but I'd rather not get there till they've left."

"I'll send a text to let you know."

"Thanks, Percy."

I put my phone away and found Leandros regarding me with his old warmth. "What?" I asked.

"That guy's in love with you, you know," he said.

I didn't like Leandros saying it out loud, or making fun of Percy in any way.

"He called to tell me the cops are searching my house. They're looking for a lottery ticket."

"Warrant?" he asked at once.

"Percy says they have one."

"Percy. What a name! How does he live with it?"

Very firmly I changed the subject: "Tell me more about this Clorinda person, Leandros. How long have you known her?"

He smiled but didn't answer. "Why are the cops searching your house for a lottery ticket?"

"I don't know."

Leandros looked at me, twinkling. "Will they find one?"

"A ticket?" I frowned, surprised. "No."

He went on looking at me. "You wouldn't be holding out on me, would you?"

"No," I answered, puzzled that he—or anyone—would think so. "Why do you think I would?"

"Don't you think that's why she was murdered? For a lottery ticket?"

"I'm not sure."

He kissed the top of my head in that affectionate, personal way that he had. "Why did she come and see you that time? Wasn't she asking your advice on whether or not she should tell her boss she had a winning lottery ticket?"

I remembered her earnest, "But can I *trust* him?"

I was lost in thought. It wasn't a ticket—it couldn't have been. She would've told me. Wouldn't she? "No."

"No?"

"She didn't mention any ticket. Her question was about love."

Deciding not to go to the fundraiser, instead I took the Lexington downtown. Percy had texted me that the police had left and he was busy putting things back in place.

The spring evening felt almost balmy, and because of my lack of sleep the night before, I was experiencing that semi-pleasant floating sensation as I walked through Washington Square Park toward Gay Street. The sky was that perfect pitch of harmony between light and dark: a luminescence that seemed to emanate from the stars themselves rather than the almost full moon that was sailing in the sky above the silhouettes of skyscrapers of lower Manhattan.

Leandros was heading back to Los Angeles early the next morning, but when we'd said goodbye he asked me to let him know how things progressed.

"And if you find that ticket, I hope I'm the first to know," he'd murmured.

I ignored his teasing. Anyway, if Amber had been murdered for her lottery ticket, wouldn't the murderer have taken it from her? How would I have gotten it?

I mulled further. Robert *had* to be the murderer. Amber herself had said he had threatened to kill her. But then why had Kathleen claimed they were together all night?

And, anyway, why would he want to kill Amber? If she had a winning lottery ticket, couldn't he've just taken it from her?

I stopped at a deli for some bright oranges and a loaf of bread. Amber had implied there was someone else in her life, not a romantic involvement, but someone. Could that someone be a news reporter who was writing an exposé about Lucky Investments?

Or was there something more criminal behind Robert's lottery 'investments'? Something for which he could be convicted?

But why would Amber agree to talk to a cop or a reporter, if she was so in love with Robert? Had she found out something about him that'd destroyed her faith in him?

Maybe he'd betrayed her with another woman.

My phone buzzed. I was going to ignore it, since I was in the midst of paying for my purchases, but something made me glance at the screen.

Robert McNeil.

Hastily, I finished paying, grabbed the paper bag, and answered as I went back outside.

"Hello?"

"Satyana." His soft voice floated through the cell phone. "I need to see you."

The light turned, and I crossed Sixth Avenue. "Can you speak up? I'm outside and there's traffic."

"Sati, where did you go after the funeral? You left so quickly. I wanted to talk to you."

"What about?"

"In person," he said. "I need to see you."

"Oh," I said. If he really was the murderer, I didn't particularly want to meet him somewhere lonely, like in a dark alley or on the roof of a brownstone. "Why?"

"I want to offer you a deal. Let's talk in person, shall we?"

"What kind of deal?"

"A business deal." He cleared his throat. "You understand, don't you? In spite of losing Amber, I still want to be friends."

I wasn't sure how to respond. I wanted to say no, I didn't, please explain. But if I did, he might think he had the wrong person and go to someone else for whatever it was he thought I had.

"Tell me more."

"Trust me, it's a great opportunity for you."

"In what way?"

"Well, put it this way. You'd make a lot more money if you give it to me than if you held onto it. Let's get together and I'll explain the process. Just be sure you bring it with you."

"Bring what?"

I heard a sharp intake of breath, and then a low whistle. "You are smart at playing dumb, aren't you?"

I hesitated. Was he talking about a lottery ticket? Had he murdered Amber for it, and then didn't find it on her body, and assumed I had it?

I didn't want to pass up any opportunity to prove it.

"I have to be careful," I said cautiously.

"Good girl." His voice softened again. "Well? Are you up for a trip to Scotland, lass? That way we can really make plans together, don't you think?"

"Scotland!" I couldn't help exclaiming.

"Yes, of course. There's nothing that can be done with it here."

"Why not?" I said cautiously, coming to a standstill under a bare sycamore in the softly-fading spring light. Did he want the ticket so he could cash it in?

He lowered his voice so I had to strain to hear. "You know that our investors are practically guaranteed monthly winnings from the Cloverleaf Lottery. You figured out how that works, right?"

"Uh-huh." Sort of.

"This is what I'm offering you: I'll bring you into the partnership. You won't make as much money up front, but in the long run you'll be much better off."

I thought fast and furiously, but spoke slowly.

"Two million dollars is a lot of money."

He sucked in his breath. "Two million? It's not worth that much, I assure you."

"Oh?"

"Not more than $100,000, at the most." He sounded agitated again. "Lass, I'll make you partner in my firm. You can make a regular income this way. You don't even have to invest yourself, we'll use the money from the other investors."

"Hmm." I started walking again. "I'll have to think about it."

"There isn't time—my client is getting antsy. If I don't give him what he's paid for, I'm going to be in deep shit. He's in Scotland, and I need to get it to him without the cops finding out. Will you bring it? I'll buy your ticket and I'll bring you to my solicitor to sign the papers. That's where our LLC is based, and I'd want to do everything legally and fairly. Ready?"

"Not really… *what*?"

"It has to be this week, lass."

"Why don't I just give it to you here?"

"There's no way I'd be able to get it out of the country," he pointed out. "But you can—no problem."

I wondered why he wanted a lottery ticket out of the country, but then I understood. As long as no one cashed in the winning ticket worth two million, he and his investors would trickle into their standard winnings that Percy had told me about earlier.

"Sorry, Robert, no can do. I've got clients scheduled all this week, and next week too."

"I think you can rearrange your schedule. This is important."

"I'm not convinced that's in my best interest."

"I think you'll agree that it is. There's nothing you can do with it here in the States, and you don't know enough about the business to make it work for you. I won't give you away if you bring it to Scotland. And in return, I'm inviting you to come on board with our Lucky Investments. A deal's a deal. Fair's fair."

 So Detective Cleveland wasn't the only one who thought I had the winning ticket. Now Robert thought so too. Truthfully, I was tempted to take him up on his offer.

Of course I knew Percy would object strenuously.

"I'll think about it," was all I said in reply. "I'll let you know tomorrow."

A few minutes later, I was inside my house. Percy had already left, and the rooms seemed back in order. I hung up my cloak and put away my purchases.

I was badly in need of a cup of tea. Today I chose Golden Monkey, a full-bodied, complex tea from China's Fujian province that I particularly loved. I had to ration this one, since it was more expensive than other Harney teas, but this evening seemed a good time to indulge. I boiled the water, steeped the leaves for the requisite four-and-a-half minutes, but even as I settled on the couch with the cup nestled in my hands, I couldn't wrap my head around Robert's phone call.

That he wanted me out of the country was obvious. That he thought I had Amber's winning lottery ticket made some sort of sense. But that he wanted me to bring it all the way to Scotland seemed ridiculously over the top.

I took the tea downstairs into my office. As I sipped, my strength and clarity slowly returned. I

gazed at the painting of Croft Moraig over the mantel.
When I'd first seen the painting I longed more than
anything else to go there, to see the rocks in person, to
steep myself in their ancient mystery.

Now as I gazed at it, I felt very little enthusiasm
about visiting. I tried to muster the old feeling the
painting had given me, but it felt dead—lifeless.

Then I realized why: It reminded me too much of
Amber. I no longer even wanted it on my wall.

I took it down, placed it on the oak chest, and put
Leandros's painting back in its place. Immediately, I
felt better.

But should I go to Scotland? I was tempted. I'd
never been there. And I knew that whatever scrape I
got into, Leandros would always be around to help me
get out of it.

And was it possible I'd be able to prove Robert had
murdered her, even if I didn't have the ticket he
thought I did? Would I be able to find out more about
Lucky Investments, maybe find out what his lottery
con really was all about?

Percy would be very interested to learn exactly
how they managed to secure regular winnings,
wouldn't he?

But as I gazed at the little painting that now lay on
its back like a helpless insect, I knew there was
something else drawing me to Scotland. Something
mysterious, and ancient, and fierce.

I wanted to visit Croft Moraig, and see the circle
that had inspired the painting I'd fallen in love with,
and spent far too much money on.

The painting that I now could hardly stand to look

at. What had changed? It was as though all the light had gone out of it. Even the beam of sunshine that had caught my eye that first time I'd seen it now looked glum. What happened to me?

 I did not relish trying to get used to driving on the other side of the road, especially by myself, so instead Percy had arranged for a car service to meet me at the airport and drive me to Halstone, where Robert's solicitors were located. He'd also booked me at a small bed and breakfast near the harbor, which, my driver assured me, was a lovely place.

"I wondered whether it would be possible to take a detour before we drive to the coast," I asked.

"Explore the city, you mean? That's a good idea."

"No, I want to go to a place called Croft Moraig. It's at the northern end of Loch Tay, near Kenmore. Do you know it?"

"The stone circle?"

"Yes. Is it very far out of the way? I was told it was about an hour from Edinburgh."

"About an hour and a half, I reckon. And then it'll be another hour and a half to get you to Crail. It's in the other direction."

Well, I wasn't meeting Robert till the next day. He'd flown me out midweek—flights were probably cheaper then. We were meeting the next morning at his solicitors' office. So I had all day to explore.

"So we can still get there by later this afternoon.

That sounds perfect."

"Sure you don't want to see something of the city itself?" he asked. "Edinburgh is so very beautiful. Have you been before?"

I shook my head. "It's my first visit. But I'll have the chance to look around this weekend. I'm not going back to the States till next week."

"That's fine then. Although the circle is very small. You aren't expecting anything grand, are you?"

I didn't know what I was expecting. Since I couldn't explain my desire to see the place in the painting even to myself, how could I explain it to a driver?

We crossed the George IV bridge, threaded our way through the city, and before long were headed north on M90. The dramatic dark clouds that always looked as though they were about to pour rain on us lowered overhead. I gazed with awe at the sheep, the oaks and ash and slender silver birch trees by the side of the highway, just beginning to shimmer with green drapery. After a while I took out my phone and took pictures as we drove. The sheer differentness of the landscape, how the hills sloped, the volcanic mesas, and the green—how green it all was after our long winter. In spite of having hardly slept on the plane, I was wide-awake, gazing out the open window as though thirsty for the sweet, moist, fresh island air.

As we drove, I began to feel an odd pull, as though I was nearing a place I hadn't seen in a long time.

"Where are we?" I asked.

"Nearing Croft Moraig. It's over there, see," he replied cheerfully. "I'm pulling over so you can take a look around."

"I don't see it."

"Easy to miss. See?"

I peered ahead. There were several other cars parked ahead of us, and a tour bus, but when I emerged and wandered up the gently sloping field toward the rocks, I felt completely alone. Stillness filled me, and as I reverently touched the ancient stones that had stood there for so many hundreds of years, I felt an ache, and a strong sense of *deja vue.*

Phone in hand, I wended my way around the rocks, avoiding the few other people there. I heard sheep bleating, and, glancing over my shoulder down the sloping meadow to where the car was parked, I saw my driver talking to a man who looked vaguely familiar.

It couldn't be.

He looked up at the same moment and our eyes clanged together in the morning sunshine which had abruptly poured through the clouds as though the light itself was made of moisture.

It was Ian.

He wore a wet raincoat and tweed hat, wellington boots, and had a large Alsatian on a leash. He looked at me challengingly, then strode toward me, the dog trotting obediently at his side.

"Thought I might find you here," he said as he neared.

I had told no one I was going to make this detour to see the stones. No one. Not even Percy. Had he followed me?

I reminded myself I was here because someone

had been murdered, and I really couldn't trust anyone.

Maybe even the driver was in some way connected with Amber's death. Anything was possible. I felt very nervous.

"Hey," I said, trying to sound casual. I reached out to scratch behind the large dog's ears—he was sitting, alert but friendly-looking, at Ian's feet, completely ignoring the sheep that milled about. Remarkably well trained.

As my heart rate returned to normal, I had to admit I was completely mystified by his presence at the stone circle.

"What are you doing here?" I asked.

"I live here, darling," he drawled. "I'm Scottish."

If he wanted an explanation about why I was there, then he was going to have to wait a while. Robert had been honest about his business. As he'd said, what Lucky Investments did wasn't illegal.

Unethical, maybe. But not illegal.

At least, not yet.

But murder most definitely was illegal. It was hard for me to picture Ian whipping out a killer knife and stabbing Amber in her gut, but …

I brought myself back to the present. Why was Ian here? Should I be afraid for my life?

I knew Percy would say so.

"Now, don't you be getting nervous," he advised me, still regarding me curiously. "I'm here to protect you, not murder you."

"Protect me from whom?"

His eyes flickered curiously, but he remained

deadpan. Really, I could not read this guy at all.

He was probably looking for the mythical lottery ticket. Maybe Robert told him I had it.

He came closer, and reached over to take my hand in his. I flinched, but then he tucked it under his arm and we walked around the stones like that, the dog trotting obediently beside us.

"Look," he said, quietly but earnestly, "This Robert's no good, darling. Really he isn't. He's greedy and unscrupulous. Stay away from him."

Maybe.

Or maybe Ian was.

 "Tell me the truth, Ian." He looked at me with an expression that would have felt chilly except for the heat in his eyes. "Why are you here?"

"Probably the same reason you are. Going after Robert McNeil."

"I'm not exactly 'going after' him," I said. "He invited me to come here. In fact, he paid for my trip. We're meeting at his solicitors' office tomorrow."

He frowned. "And why might that be?"

"He wants me to join his team. Lucky Investments."

He shook his head. "And you're going to?"

"If I have to. I want to know if he killed Amber. And if he did, I want to prove it."

"Killed Amber!" He looked appalled. "Robert McNeil?"

"Yes."

"How?"

I looked around as the midmorning sunshine glowed around us, saturating me with peace. I wished Ian would leave me alone so I could enjoy my time at the stone circle, but at the same time I felt so drawn to him. His loch-blue eyes were so deep and warm, and his hand on my arm gave me a tingle.

"Why do you care so much that he's caught? The lottery scam isn't exactly illegal, you know. Just unfair."

"About a year ago, I got involved with someone who was fairly important in the town where I used to live. It turned out he was conning me."

He looked at me. "Och, lass."

I flushed. "What?"

"I'm sorry."

"Yes, well, it's made me hate cons, scams, anything like that. I still can't believe how blind I was. And when I learned that Robert had this investment business—based on a lottery, for heaven's sake!—I got infuriated. Even Percy, my associate, was intrigued by his scheme. If he was ever conned like that, well, I'd— never forgive myself."

"All right then, and why do you think he murdered Amber?"

"Maybe because she won the lottery. If the winnings weren't distributed to his investors, his scheme would be outed. He'd probably spent all his investors' money already."

He looked at me quizzically, almost disbelievingly. "Why would he pay for your trip to come all this way? Aren't you concerned at all that he might be conning *you*?"

We'd wandered away from the stone circle, up a rocky path through the sheep meadow. Realizing this, I paused, not wanting to be out of sight of my driver. I still wasn't sure what to make of Ian.

"I don't see how, since I'm onto him."

"It's a long way to come to meet with solicitors'. Didn't you think of that?"

"Robert believes I have a winning lottery ticket that belonged to Amber. In exchange for it, he says he'll bring me into Lucky Investments as an investor."

"Ah." He sounded disappointed. "And do you have the ticket?"

"No!"

"Then what are you going to tell him when you see him? You're going to confess you haven't got the ticket?"

"I'll see what I can find. I think Amber may have found out something about the company that would get him into trouble. He might have had a strong motive for killing her."

"I don't think so."

"Why not?"

"For one thing, he had an alibi." He hesitated. "Where are you meeting him?"

"Near Crail—a town called Halstone. It's where his solicitors' office is. He wants to meet there so I can hand over the ticket and he can formally include me in his Lucky Investments business."

"So he says," Ian said darkly.

He was making me even more nervous.

"Ian," I asked, "You said you were friends with Amber. How did you know her?"

He regarded me intently. "Seriously?" he asked, as if I already knew.

"You're not going to tell me?"

"I will if you tell me where you're going to meet her boyfriend."

Glancing at my phone, I saw that Robert had sent directions for the next morning. "I told you—his solicitor's office in Halstone."

Ian looked even more disappointed in me. "So you're not going to tell me the truth?"

"That is the truth." I smiled brightly at him. "I'll be back in Edinburgh the day after tomorrow. How about if we get together for tea and I'll let you know what I found out? If anything, that is."

He grinned back. "All right then. But make it a drink instead of tea. Let me know which hotel you're staying at and I'll pick you up."

I checked in at the small bed-and-breakfast in Clunkett, then took a walk around the charming fishing village on the edge of the North Sea.

Robert and I were meeting the next day at noon. It was only a fifteen-minute taxi ride, and so I slept late and when I awoke I felt more rested than I had in a while.

I saw Robert had texted to let me know that the meeting was moved to 2 p.m. He was apologetic and hoped he wasn't inconveniencing me. I didn't really mind. Exploring the town and taking more photographs would be fun till then.

He texted again: *Suggest you walk the coastal route, you'll see some good birds and I can drive you back to the hotel afterward.*

I wrote: *Okay.*

During breakfast downstairs in the dining room, while I was sipping coffee and browsing through some touristy sightseeing brochures he texted again: *Take the walkway toward Rockway Terrace. It'll lead you to the cliff. Bit of a climb down to the beach. But worth it.*

I set off, wrapped in my cloak, which felt almost too heavy for the mild climate. I headed down the west end of the High Street and along the walkway of Rockway Terrace. After passing the high stone wall I ventured onto a dirt path which headed down toward the sea. The path continued along the coastline, crossing a bridge over a small burn and past an empty playground. At the far end it curved to the left and I took the steps up, avoiding a section of the path that looked dangerously eroded.

Squeezing through a gap in a stone wall, I found myself on a road which led to the wilder grassy shoreline beyond. Before long I was right by the windy edge of the cliff and looking out over the wild and chilly North Sea. My breath caught at its intense gray beauty.

I walked on, till I came across the narrow, rocky path to a charming cove far below. The beach was wide and lovely. In the warm spring sunshine, my cloak felt heavy and too warm. It would be nice to fling it onto the sand and lie on it.

I began my descent, cautiously at first, but once I'd

begun, the climb down was easier than I expected. The path wound between two boulders, and beyond that were more cliffs, falling into the spraying waves. I half-wished there were more people around, but I also enjoyed the close-up views of kittiwakes and razorbills that soared and rested in the sand. I clambered over seaweed-strewn flat rock, and ventured to the edge that overlooked crashing waves that sprayed me.

Exhilarated, I followed the rock to its edge, where I even saw a purple sandpiper. The terns were everywhere.

The cliffs consisted mainly of beds of Namurian shale and sandstone. I was glad Robert had recommended this hike: it was simply gorgeous. I hopped down, onto the sandy cove below that was horned by rocky outcroppings jutting into the serene sea.

A storm petrel swooped close, and veered away out to sea again. I took picture after picture.

To my surprise, a wave swept in, drenching my ankles and almost knocking me off my feet.

I looked down in astonishment, as the wave swept back out, but a moment later another one had swirled around my shins. Hastily, I climbed back on the rock. Roiling, ink-dark waves lashed around, and clambered up the rock as though trying to get to me.

The tide was coming in.

 I didn't have much time, if I had any at all. I was at least half a mile out from the cliff, and the tide was coming in much faster than I could run. Surging, roiling waves sloped up, and then pulled backward into...

I forced myself to be calm. The waves were high, but high tide was still two hours away. And it was only a forty-five minute walk to the town where Robert had said he'd meet me.

I pushed my way between two tall sheer rocks that looked suspiciously like a surge channel, eroded by high-energy waves over the course of thousands of years. The sandy path was above the reach of the waves, and from it I was pretty sure I'd be able to climb up to safety from the other side.

Another wave soaked my feet and I pressed on. I was almost through the narrow channel, and could see some small roofs in the distance, further down the coast. Almost there!

As I pushed through, I glanced up at the steep cliff to my left, trying to locate footholds to get away from the ocean. A wave snaked up around me from behind, soaking me to my thighs, and knocked me off my feet.

The next thing I knew, I was sucked into the ocean. Frantically clutching at any rock I could find, I was tumbled and scraped along until the cliff seemed a great distance away from me. The weight of my cloak had slowed the impending pull of the current in the shallows, but now I saw it as a terrifying impediment to my staying alive. I struggled to untie the hood and let it fall into the incoming wave.

Goodbye, cloak.

My phone was in its pocket. *Goodbye, phone.*

Then began a gasping, horrendous effort to try to get back to the base of the cliff. As a wave swept me closer, the prospect of being crushed against the rock face seemed worse than being drowned far out to sea.

A great wave washed over me, and I gulped salt water. Spitting and gasping, I swam madly toward land, and as the wave swept back out, I managed to clutch at a slippery rock at the base of the cliff. I made it about ten meters toward the cliff base, but then was sucked back out into frigid waves again.

I dug my toes into the sand and grasped another rock with a strength that surprised even me. Somehow, I managed to get back into the channel. Water surged around me, then sucked back out. I clung to the edges of a slippery rock, wondering if I could climb it. I was so exhausted by this time that I could hardly think, but I heard someone screaming and began to feel hopeful.

I looked around for the source of the voice, but then another wave headed toward me, surged around the rock, and I realized from the seaweed and barnacles encrusted on it that I was not safe where I was, not when the tide was fully in.

I had to get off this rock, I had to get as far away from the climbing, seething currents that surged around me, and I had to do it now.

Then I recognized the screams.

They were my own.

 Okay, the first thing to do, I reminded myself, was to *not panic*. Screaming was futile, in any case. The noise of the wind and the waves was much louder than anything I had ever heard before. No, it was up to me to get to safety. The truth was, it was unlikely I'd ever be found if I let myself be swept out to sea. Or, if my body was eventually discovered, it could be years before they figured out it used to be mine.

What would Leandros think? For a moment I imagined Leandros missing me unbearably; I wondered if he really would.

And Percy! He'd be devastated.

It was the thought of Percy that gave me the strength to move. There was no point in sitting there, now that I had caught my breath a little. I stared up at the rocky cliff behind me. It seemed sheer and slippery, but there was no other way out. The beach both to the north and the south had long disappeared under the churning waves.

The water was too cold to try to swim, even if an undertow did not drag me out to sea.

I reached up to grab a bit of rock that jutted out over my head, and tried to pull myself up. Thank goodness for yoga, which kept me flexible and strong, even at fifty. Somehow, legs flailing and arms heaving and hoisting, I managed to climb onto the ledge that protruded over my head.

I still wasn't safe from the incoming tide, though. Even here, I saw barnacles and slippery seaweed, and rocks still soaked from the previous high tide, twelve hours earlier. The ocean could still out-climb me if I got stuck.

Why had Robert advised me to take this route? Didn't he know the danger of the incoming tide? He'd been so specific about the time: *if you leave your hotel at ten you'll be in Halstone by noon. I'll meet you there.*

He must've known the tide might cut me off.

Didn't he?

Was he in cahoots with Ian? That was the real question, one that I hadn't thought about before. What if they were both in on an illegal lottery scam? And what if now they thought their game was up, they decided to do away with me? What could be more innocuous than an innocent American tourist being caught by the insidious high tide and swept out to sea? Who would ever think it was anything but a dreadful accident?

I looked up, and realized I had to get moving. I wasn't sure whether or not it was a good idea, but I decided to take off my soaking running shoes. Maybe my bare feet could grip the crevasses and pleats in the rock better than slippery rubber could. I hoped so, anyway. I left them on the ledge and gingerly stood up, pressing myself against the smooth rock. There was no way it could be climbed. I was doomed.

I urged myself to at least try to heave myself up the cliff. At this point, I had nothing left to lose. My toes found a wrinkle to press on, and my fingers found a little crack.

I moved up six inches or so. Hugging the face of the cliff like a bug, I slid my leg up until my toes found another slight bump.

Nothing surrounded me but the feel of the rock on my breasts and stomach and thighs. Nothing moved but my flesh, almost as though it were part of the rock. I felt as though we were one, the minerals, the hardness, the stern tenderness that urged me to take courage and continue to breathe. At the same time, it urged me to surrender to its crevasses and protrusions. Instead of fighting and hating the cliff that was so dangerous, I felt protected and beloved. It was offering me a stairway; it was offering me strength, a way to safety and freedom.

I was three quarters of the way up the precipice when my bleeding fingers felt a protrusion that was deeper than the rest. If my feet could reach it, my despairing arms could have a rest. But there was no way I could pull myself over to it. I knew that.

By hand-traversing left—facing the wall, fingers jammed in the crack at the back of the ledge, feet plastered against the rock just below— I kept sliding to the south, not too fast because one slip meant my doom. Amazingly, I was able to circumvent the bulge jutting over my head above me. After excruciating slowness, my feet were finally half-planted on a thin protuberance. Although I still cleaved to the rock face, my arms could rest slightly.

After a few moments of catching my breath, I took stock of where I was. Not that I looked down—that would not be a good idea. And I didn't look up, either, because my situation was so precarious it was possible that just the weight of my head moving away from where it leaned on the rock could weigh me backward and I'd plunge into the seething waves far below.

The ledge I found myself on was not wider than five inches in some places and grew narrower on either side. I couldn't climb higher because of another ledge protruding overhead, so instead I shuffled sideways, my breasts and belly still pressed hard against the rock face.

It was like walking on a narrow windowsill in the sky.

I had to look straight ahead, not down. And I had to go excruciatingly slowly.

I tried to focus on the rock, imagining it holding me, protecting me. I tried to feel the strength of it, centuries of hardness, of survival, against the relentless jousting from the waves below. I moved so slowly it was as though time stood still.

Then it began to rain.

A pale gray skua clipped past with a wild screech, followed by another. I almost let go of my tenuous hold, but recovered in time. My heart in my throat, I concentrated on keeping my bare toes gripping the rain-slick slipperiness.

I'd better keep moving.

I edged along, focusing my attention on the rock less than an inch from my eyes, and after a while I realized my heels weren't overhanging the narrow ledge any longer, but actually solidly under me. My toes were cramped from trying to grip rock, but I didn't stop. I kept moving, still gripping any crevasse that I could find, any furrow, any crease, any slight ruffle in the rock.

It seemed softer now, less stern and forbidding. In fact, wasn't that soft earth that my hands were feeling? It was hard to know for sure, since I was in a bit of a delirium by this time, but the feel of wet grass definitely made me hopeful.

Was I nearing the top? Had this slivered ledge actually led me to the top of the cliff?

I forced myself to turn my head slightly so I could see where I was heading. The ledge seemed to narrow a few feet ahead.

But the rock wasn't straight up over my head. In fact, I realized I wasn't crawling vertically any longer, but at a slight angle. And just a few feet above me I glimpsed the intoxicating sight of some sort of shrub, growing out of rock.

I *must* be near the top.

I was able to slide upward now, as the rock sloped at a more forgiving angle toward a grassy patch. Grasping the wet plants was such a relief after the slippery rock that I almost wept with joy. I went on, heaving and gasping, until finally I found myself on level ground.

Taking a moment to recover, I lay there, half-sobbing, until I realized I might die of exposure unless I got warm. I was exhausted, and the nearest town had to be at least a mile or more.

Thank goodness the rain had let up, leaving behind just a misty cloudiness. I got to my knees, and then struggled to my feet. They were bleeding and my legs felt wobbly, but they held me. I headed inland, as far from the ocean as I could, walking gingerly on wet grass and heather that felt soft as cream compared to the rocky cliff.

A narrow dirt path cut in front of me, and I skirted it because of the tenderness of the soles of my feet, but paralleled it, hoping it would lead me to a road or farmhouse. Up ahead I heard a dog barking. I'd never heard such a welcome sound in my life.

I crested the hill, wound around the edge of a field, and on the far side I saw a small blue car parked by the side of the road.

My relief made me dizzy.

A man was getting out of the car and his dog bounded toward me. I wanted to call out for help, but no sound came from my throat.

I forced myself not to pass out until I was nearer. The Alsatian approached, still barking, tail wagging. I vaguely felt we had met before. Glancing up, I recognized the man who was now striding across the wet grass toward me.

It was Ian. *Again.* For a third time, appearing seemingly out of nowhere—first in the funeral home, then at Croft Moraig, and now here.

This time, was he going to push me back over the edge of the cliff?

I passed out quietly onto the slippery tufts of wet grass.

 I awoke feeling deliciously dry and warm, enveloped in softness. From somewhere—it seemed a long way off—I heard the soothing ticking of a clock. Other than that, there was silence.

Opening my eyes, I found myself back in my bed in the hotel room, half-sitting up against a pile of pillows, snugly covered in blankets.

Sitting beside me was Ian, gazing at me, looking worried.

"Here," he said, holding out a small silver flask. "Drink this."

I extricated my hands from under the blanket, and found they were wrapped in gauze and some blood had seeped through. He held the flask to my lips. I didn't have the strength to resist, even if I was worried he might be intending to poison me. The hefty flavor of brandy wafted into my nostrils with an intensity that made me choke. I gulped and coughed, while he gazed at me anxiously.

I took another sip, more gracefully this time.

"I wanted to take you to the hospital," he said. "But the local M.D. says he's willing to come here if we need him. Cora—she's the hotel manager—and I bandaged you up as best we could. What happened to you?"

"I was walking the coast road to Halstone." I sank

back against the pillows and looked around the room. The closet door was open, as were all the desk drawers. "The tide cut me off."

"For God's sake, didn't you check? How did you get to safety?"

I gave him a brief description of my climb, but I didn't really feel like reliving it so didn't go into detail. Ian must've had an idea of what I'd been through, though, because he sat close beside me on the couch and put his arm around me.

"Poor lassie," he murmured softly. "You've been through way too much."

It was only then I realized someone must have removed my soaking wet jeans and shirt.

He read my mind. "Cora helped you out of your wet things. Everything was pretty torn up—she went out to buy something for you to wear."

"Thanks."

I sat up and kicked off the throw. My lacerated feet looked like the Little Mermaid's must have at the end of the Hans Christen Anderson fairy-tale (not the Disney movie). Looking at them, I thought how nearly I had turned into a mermaid just a few hours earlier.

"Where're your shoes, eh?"

"I left them on a ledge. It seemed easier to grab nooks and crannies of rock with my toes rather than with running shoes."

"You're the bravest lass I've ever met," he said quietly. "Do you know that people train for years before they attempt to traverse those cliffs without ropes? It's a skill very few people have."

"Wasn't skill," I returned. "It was terror."

"A fine line between the two. Now lie back and take it easy for a while. You're not going anywhere until Cora comes back."

"I'll bring you some soup. You need some sustenance."

He kissed the top of my head and then left the room, closing the door softly behind him.

I fell into a semi-stupor of blissful exhaustion. There was nothing for me to do ... My cellphone was somewhere at the bottom of the ocean, so I couldn't call anyone. My feet were too swollen to walk on ... nothing to do but lie in bed and be taken care of.

The vegetable soup was from a can, but I was so hungry I wolfed it down, along with the bread and hunk of cheddar. I drank water, but the brandy worked better at flushing the taste of ocean out of my mouth.

I dozed again.

When I woke the sun had moved around to the other side of the house, and my room was dark. I had to pee, so I wrapped the throw around me and limped painfully across the room to the adjoining bathroom.

To my surprise, Ian was at my side as soon as he heard me get out of bed.

"Everything all right?"

"Bathroom," I explained.

He supported me, waited outside, then offered to carry me back to the couch. Walking hurt, but I didn't need to be carried.

"Can I get you some tea and biscuits?"

"Yeah, that'd be great. And clothes, please. I'd like to get dressed."

"If I give them to you, you aren't going to fly away from me again, are you?"

"Why would I do that?"

"You did this morning."

"Hardly. I said I'd meet you in Edinburgh."

"*Sure* you did."

 His tone made me uneasy. His cell phone rang and he glanced at it, then hurriedly left the room. I heard his low voice in the hallway, but I couldn't hear the words. When he came back in it was some little time afterward, and he'd brought tea and a saucer of chocolate covered cookies.

He looked grim.

"Your cloak was found washed up on the shore near Halstone."

I was amazed. "Really? I never thought I'd see that again!"

He was looking at me with an expression of such puzzlement that I asked, "What?"

He folded his arms. "Were you really walking along the coast road this morning?"

I stared back. "What are you saying?"

"That story you told about climbing up the cliff... that couldn't really have happened. It's impossible."

I sat up indignantly. "You didn't believe me?"

"I didn't, no. It didn't seem possible."

I was furious. "Well, it *did* happen! I almost died!"

He looked uneasy.

"I can't believe you didn't believe me earlier! You

were *faking* sympathy!"

"Tell me again what happened," he said shortly. "You left your hotel at ten o'clock? And took the trail down to the cove? Why?"

"Robert McNeil said it would be fine to take that route. Maybe he was trying to murder me. He must have known the tide was coming in, and there was no way I'd be able to make it."

"Tell me what happened. From the beginning."

Sullenly, I repeated the course of my ill-fated hike. He listened attentively, but without the warmth he'd shown earlier. Of course, he'd been pretending before. But why?

"Why believe me now?" I said bitterly, when I'd finished. "I could have thrown my cloak off the edge of the cliff to make it look like I'd taken that trail."

"True, but there's something else that's been found that proves you're telling the truth."

"What's that?" I asked grumpily. I was seriously hurt that he hadn't believed me.

"Your plimsolls on a ledge half way up the side of the cliff."

I sat up, clutching the throw around my bare chest. "Clothes. Now."

He left, and returned with a paper shopping bag. Inside was a pair of sweat pants and a light blue acrylic sweater. My underwear—washed and dried—was neatly folded on top.

Ian left me alone to get dressed. I turned on the lamp beside the couch, since it was dusk by now, and got dressed quickly. But I felt very alone and far from home. I longed to call Percy, to hear his voice. But even if they'd recovered my phone in the zipped pocket of my cloak, it would've been destroyed by seawater.

Maybe Ian would loan me his—but somehow I doubted it. When I heard a knock on the door, I didn't respond. Ian entered anyway.

"Well, I'm an idiot," he admitted. "I thought you'd made up the whole thing about Robert sending you those texts and climbing up the cliff. But the police recovered your phone—it was in your cloak—and they've scanned the messages he sent you. You were telling the truth."

I looked coldly at him. "Who the hell are you? Why didn't you believe me?"

He pulled out a wallet from inside his Harris jacket, flipped it open, and held it in front of me. "I'm a police detective, Scotland Yard. Robert was involved in a lottery con here in Scotland two years ago, but we weren't able to convict him. He moved to New York and we knew he set up a similar lottery scam there. We contacted your police, and Detective Cleveland asked if I'd help break up his ring and put him behind bars where he belongs. We persuaded his new employee, Amber Witherspoon, to be our snout."

"Snout?"

"Informer."

It was taking me a moment to readjust my thinking. "Oh."

"And all this time I've been wondering whether you killed her."

"Me?" He shoved the wallet back in his pocket. "How could you think that? I thought you were psychic."

 "How the hell could you think I was involved in a stupid lottery scam?" I answered defensively. I could hardly remember being even faintly smitten. "And you say you're a detective."

"Well, now, lass, we all make mistakes sometimes." He went on looking at me, as though he still didn't quite know what to make of me.

I glared back. "You're the one who was scaring Amber, weren't you? I knew right from the beginning there was someone else around who was frightening her—and it wasn't Robert."

"I didn't mean to frighten her. But she was afraid Robert might find out she was snitching on him. That's different."

"Hardly. And why on earth did you think I was involved with either of them? It's absurd."

"Amber went to see you, and afterward she said she had some important information to share. I was going to meet her the day she died, but she didn't show up for our meeting. Since she said she'd discovered something right after she met with you, we thought you and Robert had some sort of connection. We saw you and him talking together that night."

"You were following me?"

"No, him. But he did hang outside your house,

waiting for you. And you talked. What about?"

"You mean the evening before she was murdered? He was worried she was in some kind of trouble. He said she thought she was dead."

"But she wasn't dead, was she? She was inside your house. What was she doing there?"

I was starting to feel very tired. "I went over all this with Detective Cleveland."

"We figured she'd discovered you were Robert's partner. She said she wanted to talk to me urgently that night."

"So then you thought I'd murdered her, so she wouldn't give me away? What nonsense."

"We didn't think you were a murderer. Cleveland talked me out of that idea. But I really don't see why you came to Scotland unless you were in partnership with Robert."

"He thinks I have Amber's winning lottery ticket, worth two million dollars."

"And do you?"

"No!" He was insufferable.

"It looks like he's been ransacking your hotel room, looking for it. Are you sure you didn't have it with you?"

"No, I never had it. But Robert thought I did. That's why he arranged to have me come to Scotland. He said in exchange for it, I could be guaranteed a regular income as an investor in his Lucky Investments."

"If you don't have the ticket, what were you going to give him when you two met?"

"I wanted to talk to him. He offered to bring me

into his business as a co-partner. I wanted to find out more about his business. I figured it might help me solve Amber's murder."

I was so mad at him by this point that every vestige of attraction vanished like dark does when it encounters light. I quietly scowled at him.

"Why does it matter to you so much to learn who murdered her?" he asked. "Why not leave it to the police?"

"You wouldn't understand."

"Try me."

But I shook my head. "I need a phone. This one in my room doesn't work." Of course, now I knew why.

"Who're you going to call?"

"I want to get on a plane home as soon as possible."

"Do you believe Robert murdered Amber? Tell me."

"I don't know."

"If he did, wouldn't you like to help us arrest him? You've gone this far in trying to prove who killed her, why stop now?"

I shook my head.

"Look, I'm in just as much trouble with my superiors as I am with you," he said, and the charm was back a little. "I might even get fired because of this."

"That's not my problem." At that point, and after all I'd been through, I just didn't care anymore, not about Robert, his lottery scam, or even finding out who murdered Amber.

All I wanted was to get on a plane back to New

York as soon as possible.

"What about you, Ian? Why do you care so much about Robert McNeil—enough to come all the way to New York to find him?"

"Before he set up his lottery scheme, he was involved in a different con. He'd promise to invest life savings of elderly people, guaranteeing that their money would be safe, and their investment would grow. He pocketed the money, paying off those 'clients' who complained with the next person's investment when he had to." His whole face had darkened. "He conned my mother out of her lifesavings, at a really bad time for us."

"Did you ever get it back?"

He shook his head. "And she died."

I softened. "No wonder you want to get him behind bars," I said, more gently.

"Come on," he cajoled me. "I think you're the only one who can help us nab him, once and for all. Where do you think he is now?"

"I have no idea. And I don't care. I just want to go home."

"I think you do care."

"Maybe he went back to the States, scamming someone else. And murdering them if they win a lottery ticket he wants for himself."

"I don't think so," Ian said. "I think he's still in the U.K. We've put out a pretty good watch at all the airports. He won't be able to leave that way without our knowing."

"Then he'll get on a boat."

"I don't think so," he repeated.

"Okay, so what's your idea?"

"He doesn't know you and I have connected, does he?"

I shrugged. How would I know?

"As far as he knows, you've drowned. That was his intention, wasn't it? "

"He wouldn't know that for sure."

Ian cleared his throat.

"I wonder whether you'd be willing to continue baiting him, just one more time."

"No, but thanks," I said. "I'd like to head back to the good old U.S. of A. on the next flight."

"Wait, please." He cleared his throat again. "I know it's asking a lot, but you're the only one who can help us nail him."

"I've done what I can—and my plan didn't work, thanks to you."

"Listen to my idea," he said. "Since Robert thinks you've drowned, we're hoping the shock of seeing you will loosen is tongue."

"He can't be sure I've drowned," I pointed out.

"Well, yes, he can." Ian cleared his throat. "We've put out a bulletin on all news broadcasts that we found an American tourist wearing a cloak washed up on the beach near Halstone. He'll hear the news, and since it's the media, he'll believe it."

I didn't like that, because somehow it made me feel extra vulnerable, so far from home, in a foreign country, with a stranger. Sure he claimed to be Scotland Yard, but what did I know about the I.D. he'd shown me? That could easily have been faked.

Worse, if Percy heard I'd drowned, all the way

back in New York, he'd be devastated. "You should've asked me before you did that. I need to call my assistant in New York and let him know I'm okay. Can I use your phone?"

He shook his head. "Too risky. We don't want anyone to know you're still alive. For one thing, it's the only way I'll know for sure you're safe. No one will try to murder you if they think you're already dead. Also, it's the only way I can think of to try to get this crook into jail."

I hesitated. "How?"

"You'll contact him, pretending to be a close friend of yours. You'll tell him you want in on his con or you'll report him. You'll arrange to meet."

"And then?"

"As I said, the shock of seeing that you're still alive may get him talking. You get him to explain exactly how the con works. How many investors, who, what, where, when. You'll wear a wire."

"And he'll try to kill me again. Great."

"If he does, we can convict him for attempted murder," Ian pointed out, "because this time I'll be there to save you."

The trap was laid for three o'clock the following afternoon. It was a good trap, as far as traps go, as long as the hunter didn't get hunted by the game, which was always possible. I was going to meet Robert in Edinburgh. I'd texted him from a fake number Ian had set up for me. He'd bought me a new phone to replace my ruined one.

Robert and I arranged to meet at National Gallery. I figured with so many people around, it was the least likely place I could get into trouble, in case Ian let me down. Not that I thought he would anymore—but I couldn't be too careful at this point.

I was flown to Edinburgh in a police helicopter, with real bodyguards, to a police station in the heart of the city, from where I was secretly transported to a quiet hotel on the outskirts of the busy shopping district. From my window I could see a tiny bit of the castle. I felt much safer being surrounded by people— even if they were strangers—and far away from those damned cliffs.

Ian had arranged for a miniature to be taped to my chest, under a cashmere scarf. He'd been unfailingly polite to me, including taking my badly damaged cloak to a dry cleaner, who'd promised to remove the stench of seawater from it before I returned to the States. But Robert had remained cool. Either he was embarrassed at his mistake, or he'd been faking his affection for me for the sake of his job.

Alone, I walked up the broad staircase to Kingdom of the Scots. I knew Ian waited behind some displays of wild wolves, but even so I was nervous. I looked at the tiny Monymusk reliquary, the Queen Mary harp, and the odd little Lewis chessmen.

There were only eleven pieces—the rest, I read, were at the British Museum in London. Dating back to the 12th century, most were carved of walrus ivory, some from whale teeth.

It was while I was relishing the sight of a berserker

rook, that I heard someone gasp my name so that it echoed through the airy room.

I turned around and found myself face to face with Leandros.

 He clutched my elbows as though he were seeing a ghost. His face was blanched and his normally laughing gray eyes seemed all blurry and reddish.

"My God, my *God*!" he cried.

All the heads of other visitors in the room turned to us.

I saw at once he was on the verge of collapse, so I spoke sternly and calmly: "It's okay, Leandros. *I'm okay.* Calm down."

"They said you were dead. Percy called—what happened?"

"Come over here." I led him to a wooden bench. Taking care of Leandros was much more important than trying to entrap Robert, even though I was sure Ian must be glaring at me helplessly from behind one of the drab drapes they'd set up for a hiding place. "Now, look, Leandros. I'm right in the middle of something here, so I don't have any time to explain. Let's meet later and I'll tell you all about it."

He was recovering quickly, but he wouldn't let go of my hand. "You're alive?"

"Yes. Look at me."

He pressed his face close to mine, as though trying to make sure. "I've had the worst day of my life. Percy called in the middle of the night to tell me you'd drowned. He wanted to come too, but I told him I'd bring your body back…" He choked, his eyes full. He looked desperate. "I took the first plane I could so I could be here with you. Just to see you again before — before—"

I knew I'd better jolt him back to his senses before he said something I knew he would regret later. "Leandros, I don't want to be buried anywhere. Everyone knows I want to be cremated. Take my body home with you! That's ridiculous."

He pulled himself together at my sharp tone. "What are you doing here?"

Quickly, I gave him a super-abbreviated version.

"I wouldn't have gone along with it except that I also think Robert killed Amber. And Ian assured me that if anyone knew I was still alive, I'd still be in danger too. That's why I didn't let Percy know."

Leandros stared at me a moment, then whipped out his phone. "Well, I'm certainly not going to let him suffer any longer than he has to. I can't believe you didn't trust either of us."

"I did," I said. "But I lost my phone in the ocean, and then Ian refused to let me use his." I glared at Ian, who'd come up to us.

"Sati—" he started to say, but I shook my head at him.

"What are you texting?" I asked Leandros.

He showed me. *"She's alive. Don't worry."*

"I guess that's all right. I don't want him to be upset. Why on earth would U.S. media report a tourist drowning off the coast of Scotland? It happens all the time."

"He was tuned into Scottish media, of course. He's been following your trek online."

Yes, Percy would be able to do that, just by figuring out where I was calling from. It was like I had a microchip in me, as long as I had my phone. When I lost it in the ocean, he probably got frantic, scoured the news, and came across the report Ian had put out in order to deceive Robert.

Poor Percy.

And poor Leandros, although I had to say, it was gratifying to see how upset he was that I was dead.

He knew that was what I was thinking, and visibly pulled himself together.

"So what now?" he asked grimly.

I introduced him to Ian, who briefly described his plan. Leandros was incredulous. "You're putting her in danger *again*?"

"We don't know for sure whether Robert knew about the tide…" Ian began.

"Bullshit," Leandros interrupted rudely.

"Anyway," I interrupted, "I'm supposed to meet him here and he's supposed to make me partner in his operation. I'm wearing a wire."

It wasn't easy persuading Leandros to let me go through with it, but he finally did, on the condition that he'd be there as well, watching from a hidden venue.

Ian objected strenuously, and maybe even a little jealously, but Leandros won.

At three o'clock on the dot, Robert showed up, smiling and bouncing a little on his heels. He looked hesitantly around the room, which had been emptied of tourists. He didn't recognize me right away when I emerged from the side of the glass cabinet the chessmen were in.

He did a double-take, but recovered, although he still looked confused.

"You?!" he stated softly.

"Surprised?"

"Yes. Glad, of course. I felt terrible when I heard that you'd ..."

I nodded gravely. "I'm okay now."

He looked around nervously. "Why didn't you tell me? Why did you pretend to be someone else?"

"I thought this was safer for both of us," I said.

"So you have it with you? Where?"

I gestured vaguely at my oversized purse, which contained a notebook, pen, tarot cards, an extra pair of gloves, and my wallet. "So tell me about the partnership you're thinking of offering me."

"Let me see it first," he said. "How did you get it? I thought you were going to bring it with you, that it was washed out to sea."

"Right, you didn't find it in my hotel room. So you would've thought that."

"Let me see it."

"Tell me first. I might not be interested."

His friendly face darkened. "You'd better be interested. I'm risking a lot by bringing in an amateur. What do you know about statistical analysis?"

"Try me."

"Yes, well. We have a bunch of investors that purchase $1,000 or more worth of tickets in the

Cloverleaf Lottery. The lottery is capped at $2 million, so if no one wins, the numbers are rolled down, and the odds are that enough numbers invested in by Lucky investors will pool together a good sum. We've been making good money for years this way. And it's legal."

"Legal?" I scoffed.

He nodded earnestly. "The lottery authorities know all about it, but there's nothing they can do. There's nothing they want to do. It's good publicity for them to see that we win."

"But you killed Amber because she found out about you?"

He cringed, eyes wide in astonishment. "I did *not*. I adored Amber. You knew that!"

"You found out she was working with the police and was going to rat you out. You murdered her."

"No, I didn't. And the lottery investment business is a scheme, not a scam. It works, and it's legal."

"You know it's not! You must've been furious when you found out the police were after you again."

He went on gazing at me, shaking his head. "Why would they be after me?"

It was only now that he seemed to be more aware of me and of our surroundings. He looked around — the room had been emptied earlier. I knew Ian and Leandros were just on the other side of the open door, but even knowing that, I felt suddenly alone.

"You know."

Then he asked abruptly: "You didn't have it with you when you fell into the sea, did you?"

"N-no."

"It wasn't in your hotel room. You have it now?"

"You mean the lottery ticket?"

Even as I hedged, I knew something was going to happen.

"What?" he looked confused.

I began to get nervous. Something did not feel right.

"I don't have it," I told him.

"You're lying."

"It's the truth, Robert."

"Amber *told* me you bought it. We know you have it. And you promised me you'd bring it here." His eyes narrowed threateningly. "Why the hell do you think I paid for this trip?"

I took a step back from his mounting fury. "Forget it, Robert. It's over. Why did you murder Amber? You're a low-level con man, and you've done pretty well for yourself, up till now. Why resort to murder?"

He shook his head, snorting like an enraged bull. "What are you talking about? I *didn't* murder her! I couldn't!"

Then he lunged toward me and seized the oversized purse that was slung over my shoulder.

Before he was halfway across the shiny floor, Ian had pounced and handcuffed him. I was impressed at how speedily he accomplished that. Leandros stood beside me, looking edgy and upset.

"So this whole thing was a trap," Robert said bitterly to Ian, as two other police officers led him from the room. "Rotten buggers."

He didn't look at me. Ian picked up my tote bag from where it had fallen on the floor and handed it to me.

"So the lottery ticket's inside this?" he asked curiously.

"I told you before," I said impatiently. "I don't have any ticket."

Leandros put his arm protectively around me, daring Ian to have anything more to do with me, ever.

"Let's get out of here," I said to Leandros. "I want to go home."

 When we were sitting in first class on the airplane, and Leandros had ordered me a sparkling wine and made sure I was comfortable, he handed me a box wrapped with a cheerful plaid bow.

"What's this?" I asked, secretly delighted. Leandros was one of the best gift-givers I knew. I had no idea what might be in this box, but images of delicious shortbread or a delightful cashmere shawl came to mind.

The box was square and heavy. I untied the ribbon and slid my finger under the scotch tape. There was a thick cardboard box inside, without a label. Mystified, I pulled apart the flaps, lifted the lid…

And there, carefully laid out in black velvet cubbies, was a complete replica of the Lewis chessmen, along with a small round chess board that became the top of the box in which the pieces could be snugly kept.

I gasped in delight.

"Oh, Leandros! It's incredible. Thank you!"

Leandros and I had a thing about chess—in fact, he'd first taught me how to play, way back in junior high. I held up a queen to the morning sunshine streaming in through the window. She sat glum and stern, her chin on a hand, staring back at me.

"Like it?"

"Love it!"

"It's not real walrus tusk, I'm afraid," he apologized. "But it was the best I could do."

"Want to play?"

"Absolutely."

We set up the small board on the tray in front of me. I opened with my knight and then decided to flank him with my other one. He brought his two middle pawns one square forward, effectively blocking both his bishops, and I felt a surge of adrenaline. Maybe *this* was the game I would finally win.

He hopped his knight over to greet me and my bishop glided forward to threaten both his knight and the sullen queen he was protecting. He brought a pawn to threaten mine; I countered with my other pawn.

"And after all that, we still don't know who killed Amber," I murmured, more to distract him from getting an advantage over me than because I thought he'd come up with any interesting theories.

"Not Robert?"

"He had a pretty solid alibi, unless Kathleen was lying about being with him."

"And not Ian."

"Did you suspect him?"

"When I saw him coming toward me after I'd climbed up the cliff I thought maybe." I stopped, seeing his expression. "Never mind. I just didn't realize he was a cop, that's all. Cleveland should've told me."

Leandros moved forward a bishop. I stopped sipping my sparkling wine, wondering about his intention. It seemed harmless enough, so I brought out mine as well.

His counterpart bishop on black came zooming forward, so that now his knight was free to move without threatening his queen. I saw it all. Where was his knight going to go, though? And when he did go somewhere, who would he threaten?

"Couldn't she've been killed by a random mugger?" he asked. "Or some angry lover from her past?"

Shaking my head, I moved my pawn to defend an empty white square, even though I didn't see much point in it. "Too coincidental. She said she was in danger."

Surprisingly, he moved his attention over to the other side of the board. I felt disconcerted.

He sipped his scotch, eyeing me with humorous glinting gray eyes, completely confident.

I wanted to win so badly, I could hardly stand it. I blinked, tried to focus. If you let yourself get angry when you're playing chess, you'll never win.

"From Robert, right?" His mind was on our conversation, not the game.

I nodded absently, concentrating on my next

move. His queen, who seemed to have been asleep, stirred. Interesting.

Don't get angry, I reminded myself. And also don't be afraid. Your job is to go for the king, to trap him, checkmate him, and end the game triumphantly. Don't worry about his queen and all the emotions she stirs in you. She's not all that threatening. *She's just a chess piece.*

"Maybe not from Robert, actually."

"Then who?"

I inched another pawn forward. "Amber came for a consultation to get something from me. She wasn't really interested in finding out about her heart's desire. What was she really asking?"

He was looking at me again, distracting me. "Yes—what?"

I glanced up, met his eyes, and then focused on the board again. "She came back the next night. She'd stolen my key... maybe that was her only purpose in coming the first time. To try to figure out a way to get back in. Robert knew she was inside—maybe she pretended to be afraid of him! Maybe he was actually out there scouting for me. I wondered why he talked so loudly when he saw me."

"Warning her?"

"Yes, maybe."

Bravely, I brought my queen forward. He brought his queen even further into my territory, so that if I moved my knight the wrong way my poor king would already be in checkmate.

Better get him to safety quickly. Time to castle.

His pawn surged forward, threatening my bishop.

Now the battle surged wildly from one side of the board to the other. It was a trick Leandros had, to keep me off guard. While I was focusing on one side, he was doing something wicked on the other.

My little bishop had to retreat again.

"And we couldn't figure out how she left that night," I remembered. "Maybe she let Robert in, left, and he bolted the door from the inside. She was too heavy to climb up the fire escape and over the roof. But Robert could easily have done that. But why? Why did he want to go into my office? There's nothing there."

"Maybe he didn't like the fact that she hadn't found what she was looking for. He wanted to find it himself." He castled smoothly.

So now I was going to have to focus my energy on that side of the board, where his queen, his knight, and both bishops were all protectively hovering around the dark king. I didn't like that.

"I just thought of something," I said. "What if Lucky Investments really is just a clever scheme, and not a con after all?"

 I looked up and found him looking at me, his eyes alight with interest. I knew he had a remarkable knack for appearing to be completely absorbed in what someone was saying, even if his mind was miles away. It served him well in the courtroom. But this time I could see he really wanted to know. "Go on."

"Maybe there's something else behind Amber's death."

"Not a lottery ticket?"

"I wonder about that. Why wouldn't she've told me about it? And if she'd hidden it somewhere in my house, the cops would've found it when they searched."

"The murderer might've taken it from her."

"But then wouldn't that person have claimed the prize money by now?"

I started to bring a pawn up to threaten his queen, but changed my mind, seeing that I'd just lose my pawn and gain nothing in return. First I'd better get my berserker rook in a good place.

Diagonally opposite, Leandros moved his rook forward one place. His motive was a complete mystery to me.

I thought I could bring my pawn up to threaten his queen now without pain. Well, just a little pain. I didn't see that one coming. First blood drawn.

Now I saw that this spot was also covered by her knight. How did I miss that? He was going to get two pawns for my one. Damn.

Well, too late now.

Not only did his knight take my second pawn, now it was threatening my queen. I moved her back hastily.

"Maybe," he said.

Time to get serious. I moved my rook to threaten his queen; his queen retreated one space. My knight galloped after her, and she retreated. But now her bishop was menacing my knight. Anxiously, I covered him with my bishop. Two against two.

But he merely brought a pawn to threaten my knight as well. That made it three to one. My horse better jump out of the way. As I leapt, I glimpsed his queen's vulnerability. I tried not to show any glee.

His queen glided gracefully to safety, just when I thought I had her.

Now what? There were dark pawns protecting every square, it seemed. There was nowhere for me to go.

"Someone else…" I pondered. "Someone else. Who else?"

"Yes, who?"

Quietly, I brought forward a rook in support of a pawn, even though it seemed a long shot. But maybe he wouldn't notice.

He moved a pawn forward to greet mine. We faced each other in a standoff.

"Kathleen?"

Wait a minute. My little pawn could grab his pawn over on the other side. What would happen if I did that?

"Who's Kathleen?" he asked.

"The receptionist who works at Lucky Investments. Amber hadn't worked there very long, but Kathleen had been there a long time."

Okay, so he protected his rook. But that still meant I could get a pawn all to myself. I brought my knight forward and captured the unsuspecting pawn.

Then I recoiled. He'd brought his queen into the fray, right between my two knights. Heart pounding, I gazed at the board.

"Yes," I mulled out loud, "she came to see me the day after Amber died. She wanted Amber's cell phone to figure out some client dispute."

"Were there texts about it?"

"We didn't find any."

"Tell me more about Kathleen."

Calm down. The game wasn't lost yet. After a few deep breaths, I realized that he'd left his queen wide open to my rook. A thrill of excitement coursed through me as I took his queen prisoner. I looked at the sides of the board, and saw I'd captured four pawns to the two that he'd captured. Not bad.

But why did he let his berserker rook remain unprotected like that? Instead, he moved a pawn... but only one place forward instead of two?

"She seemed completely neutral."

"What do you mean?"

I tried to explain. "Do you know of Jacques Lisserand, the French Resistance leader? He was completely blind, but he could sense people's auras. During the second world war, he had an amazing way of figuring out if someone who wanted to join the Resistance was actually a Nazi spy."

"Go on."

"One day a man came, highly recommended and trusted, and everyone thought he was the greatest, but Jacques couldn't get a read on him. It wasn't anything negative or spooky, it was just *nothing*. He said it wasn't worth the risk, but he was voted down. And it turned out the man *was* a Nazi. He'd gotten wind of Jacques's unique gift, and he'd practiced cloaking himself in a kind of neutral aura. For some reason,

Kathleen reminded me of that story. It was like she'd cloaked herself in neutrality."

"Like she knew you were intuitive enough to be able to see her for who she really was?"

"Maybe. But why? What's her motive?"

I looked back down at the board. Now I saw why he'd moved his pawn. If I took his knight with my rook, he'd grab my rook with his bishop. And if I took his pawn with my rook, he'd take it with his knight. Very clever.

Those pesky pawns of his were everywhere.

I retreated my knight so that my bishop had free access to the far side of the board. It was only when I made the move that I realized his knight could take mine. But instead he simply moved it out of the way. That was fine with me. I followed him, chasing him around the marble board.

Run, horse, run!

Shoot.

I'd gotten carried away and now his knight captured my rook. Not only that, but I realized he had more of my pawns. Why did I think I was in the lead just because I had his Queen? Damn—*damn* .

Well, at least I could take his knight. There.

I was getting excited. "Why did she want that phone so badly? There were lots of texts from her, but nothing damning. Why do you suppose she wanted it?"

Uh-oh, now my knight was being threatened. What was going on? The battle felt frenzied and irritating. I was getting angry again.

I retired my knight. Now it was snug in its stable

and not very useful.

"I wonder what Kathleen's relationship was to Robert?" I mused out loud.

"Just colleagues?"

Another pawn approached, meaning that my rook couldn't take it prisoner. I brought my queen as far forward as possible, protected by my bishop. If all went well, I could at least get his king into check and, if I could only think more clearly, even checkmate.

He moved his king. I swept in with my queen so we were in bed together, practically.

He retreated to the farthest square on the board and I felt a vague elation, even though I knew it was probably short-lived. With both bishops watching his king's back, I was afraid my queen might even get trapped behind enemy lines.

Now, why did he move his rook there? I wasn't sure what to do. But I couldn't resist temptation—I grabbed it.

Whew. My queen was still safe.

"Maybe. But anyway, I'm not getting involved again. I'll let Detective Cleveland do his job. It was a mistake to try to help."

A fresh rook appeared out of nowhere. *Damn.* All was lost. There was nowhere for her to go.

Goodbye, queen.

Goodbye, rook.

"Glad to hear it," he said.

The bloodbath continued: Goodbye, bishop.

I pushed a small pawn forward. He took it. More blood was shed. The dark and light squares seemed red with it.

After some intense skirmishing, I hopped my horse over to one of his pawns and nabbed it.

Oh no—my rook! What was I thinking? I was finally left with just two pawns and a knight. He just had a single pawn.

Both our pawns moved doggedly toward the opposite sides, determined to free our respective queens. I was almost there.

I had no idea how it happened, but he snuck up behind me and my king was in checkmate.

Again.

The first thing I wanted to do when the plane landed at JFK was rent a car so I could drive up to my tiny house in the mountains. My near-drowning was still so disruptive to my well-being, that I knew only a few nights spent in the heart of old mountains, hundreds of miles from the sea, would begin to heal the terror I'd experienced.

I didn't want to be afraid of the ocean… I loved the ocean. It was my friend. But that afternoon on the edge of the cliffs, that friendship had been severely tested. The mountains, I knew, would imbue me once again with the courage and confidence to face life…not to believe that I was invincible, but to know that whatever happened, I could face it with equanimity and grace.

Leandros wanted to go with me, but I refused. I knew it was important for him to get back to his extremely busy work schedule and his loving family.

We hugged, then he let me get into a taxi. He paid the driver in advance, flashed me a smile and a wave.

When I was on the expressway, I called Percy.

"I'm back," I told him. "All is well."

"Good," he said, his heart in his voice.

"I'm taking a cab home so I'll see you soon. But then I'm going to go to the Berkshires. I need to recuperate for a day or two before I go back to my consults. Can you reschedule my clients for next week?"

He said the same thing as Leandros: "Let me come with you. I'll drive you."

I was tempted. "I'll be back on Monday, I promise."

"I'll stay with my friends," he said. "Let me drive you. I'll arrange for a rental now."

I realized I wanted to be with him.

"Okay, if you're sure. Thanks, Percy."

"You want to leave right away?"

"Yes. Bring your sleeping bag—you can stay on the couch."

My need for mountain medicine was acute, and although he didn't understand why I had to go, he could tell it was necessary.

He hugged me when he saw me, which he'd never done before. I relaxed into his arms, feeling his youthful, strong devotion coursing through me so powerfully I wept a little in relief. He didn't say anything about that, but let me change, shower, and pack a small overnight bag for our trip while he went pick up the car.

During the three-hour ride, I told him about the

trip, softening my near-drowning as much as possible, and answering his questions. We stopped for groceries in Tahton, and then, as the spring sun had already begun to set, we took the long dirt road up Glass Mountain. I used to hike there frequently. It was one of my favorite places, with breathtaking vistas all times of the year and a tranquility that felt sublime. I had brought a client up there once, and she'd surprised me by designing and building a tiny house as a gift for me in return for something I'd done for her. It was the most darling tiny house you could imagine, with an orange door and the trim as pink as strawberry ice cream. A tiny metal spiral staircase led up to the rooftop terrace where I could look at the stars.

A single room with large picture windows overlooked a wide-open porch and the valley beyond. It was snuggled against the back of the mountain to the north, keeping it protected from most storms. There was a small sleeping loft over the kitchen area.

A deep well provided water that could be drawn using an old-fashioned hand-pump so I didn't need electricity. The two solar panels on the roof brought enough for light and heating water for an outdoor shower. I used the composting toilet and saw that it was doing just fine, just as Ruby, who'd designed the house for me, had assured me it would.

Percy put the groceries in the cooler, and by this time the sun had set, so I went up the metal spiral staircase to the roof to feel nestled by the mountains and to gaze at the stars. There was a lot going on, although I hadn't been following the patterns too closely, I knew that Uranus and Saturn were having arguments and Pluto was at odds with the sun. Mars was still in retrograde, which made him even more sulky than usual, but in spite of all the contentious arguments going on in the sky above me, I felt imbued by a deep, deep sense of tranquility.

I sat in one of the Adirondack chairs, snugly wrapped in a pink and violet pashmina shawl. The sky darkened, and the stars poured into the spring evening. Percy came up the stairs to join me, carrying a tray with a sparkling Codorníu and two glasses. He'd also brought slices of crusty bread, the goat cheese we'd picked up, and carrots and celery sticks.

He wore his usual blue jeans and running shoes, but he'd pulled on a cotton sweater in deference to the faint chill in the air, even though he never seemed to get cold. When he'd filled the glasses and handed me one, he sat in the wooden chair beside me. We looked at the stars for a while.

"Sati," he said in a low voice.

I glanced over. He looked so young, so earnest, but his eyes were dark and filled with intense emotion that belied his youthfulness. I knew what he wanted to say.

"It's not possible," I said, very softly.

"Why?"

I had already decided I would tell him the truth. It wasn't fair for him not to know. "Because I'm already married."

He was stunned to silence. I knew he wasn't talking about marriage—it was unlikely he'd thought that far ahead. But it was my responsibility to make him see our relationship as it really was. There was no hope for a future together. And it wasn't just our age difference. I wanted him to know that.

"Doesn't matter," he said at last.

"It does, though. If you let yourself fall in love with me, it means you won't fall in love with a woman your own age, one you can raise a family with, really grow together with…"

"It's too late," he said, almost in a whisper.

"No, it's not."

We were both silent for a long time, and then he asked, "What happened? Where is he?"

Maybe we hadn't known each other for a long time, but I felt closer to Percy than I did to anyone else in so many ways. I knew I could trust him—with my life.

"In England. He—hurt me, badly. I was in the hospital for a long time, and then I moved to the States and started my life over. I changed my name, I did everything I could to hide from him. I hoped he'd think I was dead. I figured that was the only way to be safe from him."

"Couldn't the police—?"

I shook my head. "He was extremely powerful. No one believed me." My voice caught. "That was the worst part."

"No one else knows?"

"Just Leandros. He helped me get away, set me up with my new name, a place to live. He'll never give me away. But it's why he's so protective of me."

"You don't have any family? Parents? A brother?"

"I have a sister who's much younger than me. We

were never close. And some cousins. I never let them know where I was. I was too afraid he'd contact them."

I knew Percy wanted to swear undying love to me, to promise he would never betray me, and to pour all that youthful passion over me as balm to my wounded soul, but I forestalled him. Although he was as dear to me as Leandros, I wanted to protect him from me. I knew I could not give him what he needed.

"Be my friend," I said. "Let's stay as we are."

I pointed out some of the constellations overhead and what was happening with the movement of the planets. Percy listened patiently. After a while he reached out for my hand and we sat side by side in the wooden chairs, our hands clasped, swinging gently in the starlight.

 It was past four o'clock the following afternoon when I heard the sound of a car coming up the long drive that led to my house. Percy had driven into town for some hardware he felt was needed in my house—he wanted to fix a few things. I lay on the sofa, reading and taking care of my bruised feet, even though I longed to go for a hike.

When I heard the sound of the car's engine, I assumed the car was Percy returning sooner than expected. But it was going way too fast, in a giddy, uncontrolled way. Percy never drove like that.

As it approached, I heard the strains of loud rock-and-roll music floating from the windows.

It was the music that gave me the courage to put down my book instead of lying there frozen and go outside to greet my unexpected visitors. I felt braver when I was on my feet. Surely a murderer wouldn't be playing music. Besides, only my friends knew about this house.

A small black sedan hurled itself over the last bend in the road and skidded to a stop beside my rental. With a loud hello, Brigitte uncoiled herself from behind the wheel and widened her gaze in amazement at my little house. Avery jumped out of the passenger's side and greeted me with a warm hug.

"This place is fantastic!"

I was so glad it was them and not some mad killer that I forgave their intrusion instantly.

"How did you find me?"

"We knew your house was somewhere near Tahton, and then we ran into Percy in the town!" Brigitte said earnestly, hugging me as well. "We tied him up and tortured him, and forced him to tell us where you were. He had no choice."

I believed her. Sort of. Anyway, I hadn't told Percy it was a secret where I was going.

They'd never seen a tiny house, and they had no idea how tiny it really was. I think they imagined they'd be able to sleep on a couch at least, but when I gave them the tour, which took about 30 seconds, they realized they were going to have to drive back into town and get a hotel room if they wanted to stay the night.

"Where does Percy sleep?" Brigitte asked, exchanging a look with Avery.

"On the couch. He brought his sleeping bag."

"We said we would bring you into town for dinner. He'll meet us there and then drive you back later."

It didn't make much sense to have a night on the town with my friends, since my reason for being here was solitude and recovery, but I *was* glad to see them and they were very persuasive. The salad I'd eaten earlier was long gone, and I didn't feel like having more Greek yogurt. There was a superb restaurant right on Main Street, which featured local music performers on weekends, and I was tempted.

I changed into a rust-red crushed velvet tunic and put on my boots while they talked.

"It's so pretty," Avery said. "But don't you get lonely if you're here by yourself? Good you brought Percy with you."

Brigitte winked and I smiled. I didn't really get it, because how could you be lonely with mountains like these embracing you, and conversations with the stars? At the same time, I really was happy they were there, and that Percy was staying with me.

Back in town, we found a parking place behind the town hall. It was too chilly to sit outside even though some people were trying to. But I knew what it was like in the Berkshires at this time of year. The afternoon promised warmth, but by the time the sun had set, the temperature had dropped rapidly.

Percy was already at the restaurant, seated at the bar. He gave me his seat and stood beside me while he ordered drinks for us. Conversation swirled around for a while until our table was ready.

I was wearing soft wrist gloves, but I peeled them off when my carrot-and-leek soup arrived. Both my friends gasped when they saw how puffy and swollen my hands were.

"My feet looked worse," I told them.

They both shuddered. "I still can't believe we almost lost you," Avery said.

"Let's not think about it. What really bothers me is that we still don't know who killed Amber. But I promised myself I won't get involved in trying to find out again. It's Cleveland's job."

Percy looked relieved, but Aver asked, "Is it possible she really did have the ticket? You know, the two million winning lottery ticket? It still hasn't been claimed, if so."

"I wondered that myself," I admitted. "But I'm sure the police would've found it by now."

"Unless she hid it somewhere they haven't looked."

"They are pretty good at that sort of thing," I said, doubtfully.

A friendly waiter about Percy's age approached and handed us menus. He told us the specials and happily advised us on the best sparkling wine, assuring us we would enjoy it. We ordered, but Brigitte's suggestion had got me thinking. "You mean she was killed because someone else had her ticket?"

"Is there a deadline to claiming the prize?" asked Avery.

"Yes, it's next week. But no one would be so stupid as to try to claim it now, would they?"

"Anyone can claim a ticket they've found. There's

no evidence it's stolen. No way it can be proved. Someone could even find a ticket on the street and claim the prize."

The singer launched her show on stage and we listened. She was good, but not as extraordinary as Avery was. I told Avery and she generously pointed out that they sang in different styles. She was always supportive of her fellow singer-songwriters.

During the intermission, she went over to the young woman and introduced herself. From our table, I could tell the woman was surprised and honored that Avery was at her show. I'd known Avery for so long I sometimes forgot she was well-known.

"I don't like you being alone in that remote little place with a murderer still on the loose," Brigitte said.

"Lucky no one knows about my tiny house."

"We do," she pointed out.

"Don't start freaking me out," I said firmly. "That house is one of the best things that's ever happened and I love it. Anyway, Percy will be with me."

We enjoyed our root and fiddlehead stews and tempeh treats as we listened to the second set.

"I'm as full as a tick," Brigitte finally announced.

Percy made a face and I laughed

"Are you sure you want to drive all the way back up the mountain?" asked Brigitte. "I'm sure we could share our hotel room. Two queen beds."

I shook my head.

"I don't mind driving," Percy said.

"Let's meet for breakfast though, okay?" I said. "And then we'll take you on a hike. A short one, because of my feet."

They were both enthusiastic, and the weather promised to be very fine.

When Percy and I arrived back home early on Monday afternoon, I headed out almost immediately to visit Judy. I hadn't seen her in over two weeks, and she'd asked me to pick up a few groceries. I was there a couple of hours, recounting an abbreviated version of my adventures, then took a crosstown bus back. My feet were sore from hiking the previous day.

Percy was in my office, washing the tall window, when I returned. He jumped down from the sill, a cloth and spray bottle in each hand.

"I did some cleaning up in your office. Thought it needed some freshening up."

He came over to me, his face bright. I noticed the floor had been polished and smelled the lemon oil. Things did look more neat and shiny.

"It looks great," I said warmly. "Thank you so much."

"I found something," he said.

"What?"

"Amber's winning lottery ticket, worth two million dollars."

 Okay, that was not what I'd expected.
Amber's winning lottery ticket.
In my office.
"Where was it?"

"She must've shoved it under the vase on the mantel. We don't move it very often."

It was a Chinese vase, containing a few dried grasses and hydrangeas, artfully arranged so that I didn't have to fix them. The vase was fragile and rare, and I dusted it but rarely moved it.

"That's crazy. Did you call Cleveland?"

"Waiting for you."

"You're sure it's a winning ticket."

"Yep—two mill."

We looked at each other. The way the Cloverleaf Lottery worked, all you needed was the ticket itself. You just showed up at the lottery headquarters in Brooklyn with the ticket in your hand and hoped you weren't mugged on the way.

People who won were usually pretty quiet about it until they'd claimed their prize.

Because the ticket was literally like having millions of dollars in cash in your pocket.

I didn't like the feeling at all.

"How did it get there? The police searched every corner of the house."

"Right."

"So Amber couldn't have put it there. The cops would've found it."

"I know."

"Well, who's been here since then? Who could have put it there?"

"I've made a list of everyone who's been in this house since the police were here." He handed me his phone and I squinted at the screen. There were only five names there: Brigitte had dropped by to say hello,

Cleveland wanted to see me, my weekly grocery delivery, a walk-in potential client called Justine, and Kathleen Jones.

"What did Kathleen want?" I asked.

"To talk to you."

"She must've known I was in Scotland."

"She showed up the day I thought you'd drowned." His face was red. "I told her you were dead."

I let him compose himself and then pressed him. "How'd she react?"

"Couldn't say."

"Did you leave her alone at all?"

"Just for a sec. She asked for water. And I—"

Yes, he would've wanted a moment to get his emotions under control. He must've gone upstairs, gotten water for them both …

"So Kathleen could've put the ticket there, trying to frame me for Amber's murder. Think she had time?"

"Probably."

"Where is it?"

He took it out of his front shirt pocket and handed it to me. It was green, as they all were, and the numbers were stamped on its face in fuzzy black ink, as though from an old-fashioned stamping machine.

Why would Kathleen want to frame me, though? To protect Robert? Had she lied about their alibi?

What was their relationship?

Were they in love?

Or… had they been in love and then Robert had fallen for Amber?

And Kathleen was riddled with jealousy?

"I think she was the one who let Amber out of my house that night," I said suddenly. "Maybe she thought Amber had hidden her lottery ticket here, and she stayed behind to look for it. She didn't find it, and maybe she saw Robert on the stoop again? So she escaped out the back. She's tiny—she'd have no problem climbing the wisteria."

I went on looking at Percy, everything falling into place like a waterfall crashing down the side of slippery black rocks, roiling through rapids, and then finally reaching sunlit clarity.

"I'll call Detective Cleveland," Percy said.

"No, wait." I examined the ticket again. "Hold it."

He paused, reluctantly.

"Get one of the tickets you bought for us. Still have it?"

"In the trash."

"Let's see it."

He returned a moment later with the ticket. It was the same pale green as the one I was holding, with the small cloverleaf on the left side, the grinning, winning smile in its leaf-framed face.

But the numbers were printed onto the ticket as though by a machine.

The numbers on the one Amber had hidden on my mantel had a smeared depth, as though they'd been stamped with an inkpad.

Laser printing versus ink...

"Find out from Cloverleaf what kind of ink they use on their tickets," I said, although I already knew. "And whether they always print them the same way… and where."

Percy returned to his desk, and I heard him making the call. I went on gazing at the two tickets, wishing with all my heart I was still intuitive enough to be able to see exactly what had happened in the making of the second one.

Two million dollars! I was holding two million dollars in my hand.

But it didn't feel like that. It felt like a tiny piece of heavyish paper on my palm.

I turned it over, as though it were a dead butterfly I could bring to life with my breath.

No such luck. It felt deader than dead.

Just like Amber.

Percy returned. "Laser printer, in Little Rock, Arkansas. They gave me the whole trip of how they're transported to headquarters…super security. I can tell you, if you're interested."

"No chance of interception?"

"Unlikely."

"I think this one's a fake. It's inkjet, not laser. Whoever made it tried to copy the original ticket, but it got slightly damp under the vase. See how it's smudged?"

Percy came over and studied the ticket carefully. It had been faked so well that he took it over to the window to see it more closely.

"So who has the real one?" he asked, handing them back to me.

Now it finally *really* all made sense.

I smiled at him. "I don't believe there is one."

 We went into my office and I picked up the painting by McCoy Brown of Croft Moraig that still lay on its back where I'd left it. I studied it, shook my head in astonishment at my own obtuseness, and then handed it to him.

"Take a look."

"What do you mean?"

Gingerly, he took it from me and studied it. "What about it?"

"Look on the back. See the price?"

"999.99. Euros, right? Or is that pounds sterling?"

"Euros. Amber thought they were dollars."

"You paid $1,000 for this?" he demanded, shocked.

I took the painting back from him, in case he was tempted to punch it. Sometimes he was overly protective of my finances.

"That's a helluva lot of money for a piece of art," he grumbled.

"I know. But you know what? This is not the painting I bought. I get it now. It's a fake. That's why I lost interest in it. The original gave me such a feeling—it's hard to describe."

He rumpled his hair in exasperation, not comprehending.

"I bet the original is worth one hundred times what Amber sold it to me for. I bet she sold me the wrong one. Let's go check."

Within moments he'd looked up the artist.

"Oh my God," he said, turning pale.

We looked at each other. "So this painting is actually worth half a million?"

"Yes. It probably never occurred to her that a painting could be so valuable. She'd only just started working there, remember."

"And Robert was furious when he found out—but why not just ask for it back?"

"My guess is that he's dealing in art that's under the radar. He may not even legally own this painting."

"Then how did he get hold of it?"

"Might be on loan—or a temporary exchange with another gallery. Or maybe he does own it outright, but he didn't want to draw attention to himself because the gallery is just a front for Lucky Investments."

Percy was nodding. "I get it. Amber made an appointment to see you but in reality she just wanted to get the painting back. Robert must've persuaded her—or threatened her."

"And when she was here, she couldn't figure out a way to, so she took the key, intending to sneak back in and replace it with the copy."

"But when she came back, it still wasn't here—remember the framing company got backed up. So who let her out? Robert? And did he murder Amber when she didn't produce the painting? Is that logical?"

I grinned at him. "Murder's not always logical."

"There has to be a better motive."

"I agree." I reached for my cloak. "Call Detective

Cleveland?"

"Wait, where are you going?"

"To the gallery. I get it now. Robert wanted me to bring the painting to Scotland. I thought he was referring to a lottery ticket, but it was the painting he wanted. That's why he tried to grab my tote bag in the museum. He thought the painting was in it."

"So who do you think has the painting now?"

"Kathleen Jones?" I ventured.

"Then I'm coming too."

"Stay and call Detective Cleveland instead. I think I might be able to get her to tell me the truth if I'm by myself."

 The sky was low and dark. A few large drops fell on my nose when I emerged from the subway station and headed toward Front Street. The building seemed almost eerily quiet, even though it was open.

Kathleen was seated behind the desk, but she gave a start of surprise when she saw me.

"Robert's not here," she said frostily. "You'll have to schedule another time."

I replied affably, "I came to see you."

"What do you want?"

"You have the real McCoy, don't you? I finally figured it out."

"I don't know what you're talking about."

"You realized Amber had sold me the real thing, instead of the fake. You and Robert told her she'd better get it back or she'd be fired. She was scared, and she needed the money. When she came to see me for a consultation, she couldn't think of a way to get the painting off the wall. But she was clever enough to grab the spare set of keys I leave in the basket by the front door."

Kathleen glared sullenly but did not speak.

"She came back the next night to get the painting. She was actually afraid that Robert had found out what she'd done, and she thought he might kill her. She wasn't making that part up. But I finally realized who let her out. There's no way she could've climbed up the wisteria to the fire escape from the garden. She was too large. But you could have. Easily."

"I don't know what you're talking about," Kathleen muttered again.

Her seeming docility gave me the impetus to go on.

"You took the painting with you, didn't you? And replaced it with the fake. It never occurred to me, or I would've realized why the painting meant nothing to me after Amber's murder. I thought it was the connection with her that made me feel odd about it. But no. It wasn't that. It was that it was a fake."

"You're crazy."

"What's crazy is that Robert doesn't know you have the painting! He thinks I have it… that's what he wanted me to bring to Scotland." I laughed out loud. "And I thought it was a lottery ticket."

She did a funny thing then: she shifted from glare, and sullen denial, to her former neutral zone that had puzzled me so much when she'd been in my office. I couldn't get a read on her.

It was strangely disconcerting.

"I've been wrong about everything, right from the start," I shook my head at myself. "I thought you were in love with Robert. I had no idea you were holding out on him."

She twisted her lips and burst out: "I do love him! I do! I hate that bitch—when he told me he was going to take her away with him I wanted to kill him."

"But instead you killed Amber," I said quietly. "You had opportunity and motive—of course. It was you."

"What? *No!*"

"I see what happened. You let Amber out of my house and said you'd take the painting and give it back to Robert for her. But instead you kept it. You told them both it was still in my house, even though you'd actually replaced it with a fake. What was your plan, Kathleen? Were you going to try to sell it yourself?"

She went on glaring.

"You must have told Amber to meet you at my house, to bring the key, and you'd get the painting. But you killed her instead. And then you wanted to frame me for her murder by leaving a pretend lottery ticket in my house for the police to find. That was amateur of you. When we saw it was a fake ticket, the whole thing fell into place. I realized why the painting I'd loved so much meant nothing to me now. It's because it was a fake. You'd already replaced it with a fake. You have the original."

She made a jerky movement, and before I could

blink I saw a knife in her hand.

Then she lunged at me, street knife held expertly in her right hand. Luckily I was half-expecting her anger to overcome her good sense, and easily sidestepped the clumsy maneuver. As I did so, I whipped out my cloak to receive the knife instead of my torso. The wharncliff grind of the Raven ripped through the lining.

Even in the urgency of the moment, I was upset about my cloak: just when it had been so carefully dry-cleaned and all the seawater and seaweed stench had been removed. Now it was going to have to be repaired again.

Still, there was no time to worry about my cloak now. Kathleen's pinched, white nostrils were flaring like a bull's, and her rage seemed a cloud around her that distorted reality. I'd better try to get her under control.

"Cool down," I ordered her, using my Voice.

Unfortunately, she seemed too far-gone to even hear me. She advanced toward me, the steel crusher glinting in the slanting rays of the spring sunshine that had just emerged from behind the dark rainclouds.

 I heard voices in the foyer behind me, but didn't dare turn my head. At any instant, she'd leap again and I'd better be ready. I heard police sirens in the distance too, and vaguely hoped they were heading in my direction, but why would they be?

Unless Percy …

Footsteps pounded up the stairs.

"Hold it!"

Completely ignoring the peril of the evil-looking knife, Percy leapt on the crazed woman and twisted her arm backward until she dropped it. Then he forced her to the ground, face down, his hands clenched around the back of her neck. He was panting hard. Had he run all the way here from Gay Street?

He glanced up at me, his eyes furious. "You okay?" he demanded.

I nodded, too stunned by his sudden appearance and my near-miss to do much else. Moments later, Detective Cleveland came crashing through the front door. Within seconds he and another police officer had relieved Percy.

She stayed silent, glowering, not so neutral any more.

"Give her her rights and take her downtown," Cleveland sharply ordered the officer.

The police officer began the routine as he led her out the door to the police car parked at an angle. Another car had drawn up too, and the blue lights kept swerving around the room where we stood.

Cleveland glared at me, and so did Percy, and I put up my hands in a protective gesture. "Why are you so mad? It looks like I got you Amber's murderer, didn't I?"

"You could've been killed!" Cleveland shouted. "Why didn't you tell us about her, rather than confronting her yourself?"

"What happened, Sati?" Percy demanded, but

more quietly. "Tell us."

I leaned against the desk, realizing I was a little dizzy.

"I didn't realize she was the murderer until just now," I said contritely. "If I had, I wouldn't have come, of course."

"How do you know she's the murderer?"

"Because of the painting. Now I see exactly what happened that night Amber came to my office. Kathleen knew how valuable it was and replaced it with a fake. A good one, but no wonder I didn't care for it after that."

"But why did she kill Amber? If she had the painting that doesn't make sense. "

"Kathleen and Robert were lovers. She was crazed with jealousy when Robert began dating Amber."

"How the hell did you find that out?" Percy demanded.

"She told me."

"You're kidding!"

"Yes, and she's the one who let out Amber that night, but she stayed behind...to get the painting. She probably told Amber she didn't have it, so Amber must've told Robert I still had it. And he wanted me to bring it to Scotland. He wanted it out of the country. He knew he could sell it for a lot more in Europe than in the U.S. Lots of people haven't even heard of McCoy in this country."

"And you thought he wanted you to bring the lottery ticket."

"Yes, I misunderstood that."

"But the motive for the murder wasn't a lottery

ticket and it wasn't an expensive painting. It was love."

"Let's call it crazy passion," I corrected him. "Not love."

"And to think of Amber and Kathleen both downstairs in your house, while you were asleep, I can't stand that…" Percy shuddered.

He looked so distraught I tried to distract him with another task.

"My cloak got torn. Look at it. I'm going to have to get it mended." I held out the side of the cloak so he could see the huge slash in the lining that Kathleen had made with her knife.

Instead of getting practical, however, he blanched even more as he realized the danger I'd been in.

"Percy," I said firmly. "I'm *fine*. Let's go grab some lunch." I smiled at Cleveland. "Won't you join us?"

Winslow Eliot is an award-winning author of fifteen books of fiction, non-fiction, and poetry. Her work has been published in twenty countries and translated into eleven languages. Like her heroine, Winslow is an intuitive consultant who reads cards, stars, and palms, and loves a good mystery.
Find out more about her at winsloweliot.com.

www.ingramcontent.com/pod-product-compliance
Lightning Source LLC
Chambersburg PA
CBHW032002170626
46807CB00006B/2604